Wanted: UFO

Wanted: UFO

by Beatrice Gormley

illustrated by Emily Arnold McCully

DUTTON CHILDREN'S BOOKS   NEW YORK

Library of Congress Cataloging-in-Publication Data

Gormley, Beatrice.
    Wanted, UFO / by Beatrice Gormley; illustrated by Emily
Arnold McCully.—1st ed.
        p.   cm.
    Summary: Fifth-grader Elise is thrilled when a UFO appears
in her friend Nick's backyard but shocked when she discovers
why its occupants have come to Earth.
    ISBN 0-525-44593-5
    [1. Extraterrestrial beings—Fiction.   2. Science fiction.]
I. McCully, Emily Arnold, ill.   II. Title
PZ7.G6696Wan   1990   89-26017
[Fic]—dc20   CIP
                                                         AC

Published in the United States
by Dutton Children's Books,
a division of Penguin Books USA Inc.

Published simultaneously in Canada by
Fitzhenry & Whiteside Limited, Toronto

Designer: Nancy Goldenberg

Printed in U.S.A.   First Edition
10 9 8 7 6 5 4 3 2 1

to Ann Durell,
for her encouragement,
insight, and excellent advice—
for teaching me how to fly

Contents

-1-

UFO over Rushfield

It was a clear April evening, the night Elise Hall went out into her backyard to watch for UFOs. She didn't really expect to see any, but watching for UFOs was part of the research plan she had turned in to Mrs. Curley.

Besides, Elise wanted to get out of the house and get rid of the pictures that were haunting her mind. She had just watched a TV program about a boy in India who was brought up by wolves until he was ten. Then he was captured by some villagers and taken to an orphanage, where they tried to civilize him.

It was no use. All the wolf boy wanted to do was go back into the forest to live. But the people at the orphanage didn't understand this. They kept trying to get the wolf boy to repeat a word or to stand upright. And he just ran from corner to corner of his pen on all fours, whimpering and growling.

1

"Wasn't that a fascinating program?" Elise's mother remarked.

Lewis, Elise's older brother, raised his head and pretended to howl. "Now can I watch something good?"

Mr. Hall, reading a magazine, didn't say anything. Neither did Elise, because she felt sick.

Fascinating? thought Elise now, as she took deep breaths of the cool night air. That program was the most awful thing she had ever seen. Even working on a science project was better than thinking about the poor wolf boy.

Elise had been putting off the rest of her research because she was sorry that she'd said she would do her science enrichment project on UFOs. She liked to think about people from the stars and make up stories about them, but research was something else. She'd looked through three books by people who said they'd visited UFOs, and they were all really stupid stories about lying on tables and being poked by gray-faced little men. These books made visiting a UFO sound like going to the dentist.

Standing on the lawn with her head back, Elise began to realize this wasn't a good place to watch the sky. She could only see a sprinkling of stars between branches—the tall pines around the Halls' yard blocked out most of the sky. A UFO could scoot along the horizon only a few blocks away, and Elise would never know it.

She walked around the house, across the front lawn, and onto the gravel road, Twin Ponds Lane. But pine branches crossed the sky above the road, too. Where could she find a big open space for sky-watching?

Elise hesitated, pulling up the zipper of her jacket against the clear, chilly air. There was the playing field at school, but that was too far to go at night. Oh—the golf course. That was a good open place, and it was just up the hill.

Elise followed the short gravel road past Mr. Russell's small house and between two ponds. Past the ponds, a path led through more pine trees to the top of a hill. Being out by herself at night gave her a pleasantly secret feeling. The sky was lighter, against the black trees, than she would have expected. She couldn't see much, though, except from the corners of her eyes. But she heard the peeping chorus of tree frogs, and she smelled the pines and the duck ponds.

Stepping onto a flat circle of grass, one of the golf course greens, Elise paused. She heard the warbling hoot of a screech owl, like a warning. At the same time, she saw a red glow on the opposite hill, at the other end of the fairway.

Elise felt a tingle of excitement. There was probably some ordinary explanation, but until she found it out, the mysterious red light could fit into an interesting adventure. Sneaking through the pines, along the cart path, Elise turned on the tape she ran in her head:

For some time the girl had sensed that her star family was trying to contact her. Now, gazing toward the mysterious red light that was too small and steady to be a fire, she felt vibrations in tune with her very being.

In a flash she understood the purpose of the light. It was meant to draw her, the lost child of the stars, to-

ward the rendezvous spot, and at the same time signal the starship to—

A movement caught the corner of her eye. Elise stopped short, holding her breath. There was some-one—or something—else on the golf course. She heard puffing, and she saw a faint shape against the black-on-black of the shrubs and pine trees. Suddenly the night didn't seem so cozy, and Elise wished she had told her parents where she was going.

"Any more shooting stars, Nick?"

Elise let out her breath. That was not an evil voice, or even an alien voice. It was the voice of nice Mr. Russell, who lived down the road from the Halls. He was puffing on his pipe.

"Not yet," came a calm, confident answer. That was Nick Russell, one of the boys in her class.

Now that Elise knew they were there, she could make out the shapes. There was Nick, a tall, solid boy, with his head tilted back, holding binoculars to his eyes. And there was his grandfather sitting on a bench near the tee. The mysterious red light was a flashlight with red tissue paper over it, so it wouldn't be too bright. Thank goodness she hadn't screamed!

At the same time, Elise was a little disappointed. "Hi, Mr. Russell," she called, walking out of the pine trees. "Hi, Nick."

"Elise? Well, hello there, sweetheart!" Mr. Russell called back. "Are you going to join Project Meteor-Watch? Nick's spotted a couple already."

"She's doing a different project," came Nick's voice out of the dark. "UFOs."

4

Mr. Russell laughed. "UFOs! Flown by intelligent aliens, huh? Let me give you a better research topic, Elise, something I've always wondered about: Is there intelligent life in Rushfield?"

"Speak for yourself," Nick teased him.

His grandfather laughed again. "Say, Elise, do you know why golfers always carry a second pair of pants?"

"I just told him that riddle," said Nick. "It's in case they get a hole in one."

Elise laughed politely, although she had heard Tim Perillo tell Nick that riddle yesterday. She wondered whether it was all right for her to stay here to watch for UFOs, or whether Nick would rather have her go somewhere else.

"Whatever you're looking for," the older man went on, "why don't you sky-watch with us? Nick's got a star map and binoculars. Nick, let Elise have a turn with the binoculars." Sitting back down on the bench, he began to fiddle with his pipe.

"She's not going to see any UFOs anyway," grumbled Nick. "Hey!" he warned Elise. "Watch out—you almost stepped on the flashlight." But he handed her the binoculars.

Elise wasn't sure the binoculars would help either. "UFOs are supposed to be big enough to see without binoculars," she said. "Some of them are as big as football fields, in fact."

"You might as well look in Lyra," said Nick. "That's where all the meteors come from, this season. Hey, there's one. That makes three. Grandpa, did you see it?"

"Yes, I certainly did," said Mr. Russell, with his pipe in his teeth.

Peering through the binoculars, Elise had missed the meteor. "Look in where?" she asked.

Nick sighed as if he thought Elise didn't know anything. But he showed her how to find a constellation, shining the red-covered flashlight on his star map. "You start with finding the North Star, Polaris. Well, actually, first you find the Little Dipper, here, and the Big Dipper, and that's Draco the Dragon in between." His cool voice was almost like an adult's. "If you keep looking up at the stars," he added, "pretty soon it seems like you're floating around up there."

Elise gave him a surprised glance, but it was too dark to see his face, and his voice was still calm. She hadn't thought Nick Russell was the kind of person who would imagine himself floating among the stars.

"Do you want to find Lyra or not?" asked Nick. "We're probably missing a lot of meteors. Hey! There goes another one. That's four."

Elise pressed the binoculars to her eyes, fiddling with the knob in the middle to focus them. She kept going past the clearest focus.

Nick went on, "You can't see Lyra very well because it's almost below the horizon. Just look at the Little Dipper and then sort of to the right."

Hearing Mr. Russell snorting gently from his bench, Elise wished he were the one showing her how to sky-watch. "The sky doesn't really look like the star map. There's a lot of extra stars up there," she remarked. "I can't even find the Little Dipper now."

"You're the dip," said Nick. "You've turned south, and the Little Dipper's in the north. Turn around."

"How was I supposed to know where north is?" Elise didn't think she was stupid, but Nick was making her feel that way. She lowered the binoculars. "Besides, this focus thing is driving me crazy."

"If it's driving you crazy, you must not have far to go," said Nick. "Just turn it a little at a time, like—"

"Here, you take them." Feeling her cheeks grow warm, Elise shrugged the binoculars strap from her neck and held them out. Nick probably thought she wouldn't notice a meteor if it fell on her head.

"I was just showing you what to do," said Nick reasonably. But he didn't seem sorry to have the binoculars back.

Just as he took them, something bright appeared in the northern sky. The shining dot glided above the golf course, seeming no higher than a hot-air balloon.

"Look! Look at *that* meteor!" Elise felt proud. That was a really bright one, and *she* had seen it first.

At her shoulder, following the dot with his binoculars, Nick made a strange sound, "Uhh." As if someone had punched him in the stomach.

Maybe it was Elise's imagination, but the bright dot seemed to hang right above them for a split second. Then it streaked for the horizon, hovered another instant, and sank out of sight.

"Where did it go?" Nick was searching the sky frantically. "Where is it?"

"Whoo-ee!" called Mr. Russell. "That one would be worth ten regular ones, if it were a meteor. But it

must have been a plane in trouble, the way it was moving."

For a moment Nick didn't say anything. Then he repeated in a choked voice, "Where did it go?"

"That way," said Elise, pointing to the pines at the edge of the golf course.

"Right toward *my* house." Nick's voice had sunk so low that Elise could hardly hear him.

"You're right!" Mr. Russell chuckled. "Your house is on that edge of the golf course. If we went over there, we'd probably see a big, smoking crater where your house used to be. A little surprise for your mom and dad when they get back from Bermuda."

But Nick didn't laugh. "Can we go see? We could get your car and drive over there. Come on, let's go."

Elise looked at him in surprise. What was he so excited about?

"No." Mr. Russell spoke firmly. "You didn't believe what I said about a crater, did you, Nick? You aren't really worried about that?"

"I guess it couldn't have been a meteor," said Elise, "the way it stopped for a second and then started again."

Nick stared at Elise. Then he spoke to his grandfather. "Okay, then I'll walk over there myself." He took a few steps across the grass, but his grandfather grabbed his arm.

"What's gotten into you, Nick? Calm down." Mr. Russell put an arm around Nick's shoulder. "Look, the plane or whatever-it-was disappeared in the *direction* of your house"—he pointed at the black peaks of the pine trees in the distance—"but that doesn't mean it landed there. We didn't hear any crash. There's nothing to go see."

Nick wasn't calming down. He was flicking his red-shaded flashlight, stalking around the green. "Please, can't we go just to check? What if—" He stopped, as if he didn't want to say out loud what he was thinking.

Elise looked curiously at Nick, but she couldn't see his expression in the dark. "I don't think it was a meteor," she repeated.

"Neither do I, sweetheart," said Mr. Russell. He knocked his pipe against the bench leg and stood up. "Well, have you kids had about enough stargazing? You told me to keep track of the time, Nick. That would make four meteors you sighted in half an hour. Not counting that last thing."

"Right," said Nick. He had finally calmed down. In fact, he sounded dazed.

"*I'm* going to count it as a UFO," said Elise. She felt cheerful. This part of her research, at least, hadn't been so bad.

"Why not?" Mr. Russell patted her shoulder. "It *is* unidentified, as far as we're concerned. Now, Elise, you come along with us. Did your mom and dad say you could walk up here by yourself? They must be wondering what in the blue-eyed world happened to you."

Following Nick and his grandfather down through the grove of pine trees to the ponds, Elise picked her way over roots and fallen branches. She remembered something she had read about a woman who had seen a UFO from her backyard. The woman had thought, I wish it would come closer, so I could take a good look—and the UFO had floated toward her until it was right over her lawn.

Elise should have tried that with the bright dot—*her* UFO. That would be the kind of research that Mrs. Curley liked to see in a report, whether it worked or not. Only the bright dot had come and gone so fast, Elise hadn't had time to think of it.

Ahead of her on the path, Nick was trying again to talk his grandfather into driving over to his house. "Just drop it, now, Nick." Mr. Russell sounded annoyed.

Why was Nick so anxious to find out where the bright dot had gone? I'd rather *not* know where it went, thought Elise, because then it wouldn't be a UFO anymore.

Elise smelled the freshwater smell of the pond at the bottom of the path. Over the peeping of the tree toads, she heard Mr. Russell tell Nick, "I said no. Don't ask me again, or you can forget about going to the planetarium this weekend."

E-loose

When Elise walked into the classroom the next morning, a group of boys and girls was gathered in the middle of the room like a flock of geese, their necks stretched upward. Mrs. Curley had clipped their new papers onto the clothesline hung over the desks.

Uh-oh, thought Elise. Her heart seemed to flip into her throat. Ever since she had written that paper last week, she'd been wondering if she'd made a big mistake.

"I've Got a Secret" was the topic the teacher had given them, and Elise had taken a chance and written about a real secret. Well, it wasn't exactly real, but it was something she liked so much, she probably shouldn't tell anyone about it. And now Elise's secret was hanging up in the middle of the classroom for everyone to see. Everyone, including Rosemary, who loved a chance to make fun of someone.

Elise's best friend Carrie caught sight of her and motioned. "Come and look what *you* got, Elise!"

Elise let her book bag slide onto her chair and hurried to join Carrie. But she guessed, from her friend's wide, dimpled smile, that there would be a red A at the top of her paper. Full of relief and pride, Elise smiled back.

Elise had worked harder than usual on this paper—for instance, putting in those two pictures. One was her school picture. The other, from the cover of a paperback book, showed a man and a woman and a girl on another planet. All three of them had wild, bushy hair like Elise's and big dark eyes.

"Where do you get those ideas, Elise?" asked Carrie. "All I could think of for a secret was where my old hamster was buried in the backyard. I mean, I guess I could have written about Judd liking me, but—" She broke off, giggling and rolling her eyes at the silliness of that idea.

" 'I Came from a UFO.' " Behind Elise, Rosemary read the title of the paper and snickered. "I might have known Elise came from outer space!"

As the other kids laughed and jostled to get a better look, Carrie turned to Rosemary. "I'd rather come from outer space than crawl out from under a rock like you."

But Elise didn't want to get into a fight. "Look," she said quickly, pointing to the paper clipped next to hers. "Nick got an A, too."

Nick Russell was gazing up at the grade on his paper with calm satisfaction. Next to him his friend Tim Perillo read aloud, " 'My Ambition—Astronaut.' Hey,

Nick, that's a cool picture of you in your NASA shirt."

Elise was feeling friendly toward Nick from sky-watching with him and his grandfather last night. But now she noticed a little frown on Nick's face as he ran his eyes over her paper. Tim read Mrs. Curley's comment slowly, as if it were a joke: "Very imaginative, Elise!"

Flushing, Elise went to hang up her jacket. Maybe Nick and Tim thought Nick was the only one who should get A's—well, he wasn't.

As the bell rang, Mrs. Curley clapped her hands for attention. "You all know what that bell means. Tim, did you want to teach today? Maybe you could give us lessons in making faces."

"Sure," said Tim cheerfully. "Here's how."

As Elise and all the rest of the class turned to see what Tim had been doing, he pretended to twist his ears forward, as if they were knobs. At the same time, he made a cranking noise and pushed his tongue slowly out of his mouth.

"That will do, Tim," said Mrs. Curley.

But Tim punched the tip of his nose, as if it were a button on a machine, and his tongue zipped back inside his mouth with a *boinng*.

The teacher ignored the giggles and clapping for Tim's performance. "Let's start today by sharing, those who are doing science enrichment projects, what we've discovered so far. Let's see—Elise, your topic is UFOs. Have you turned up any interesting facts?"

Elise sat up straight. "Yes! I saw one last night. I think."

"My!" Mrs. Curley opened her eyes wide. "Did all of you hear that, boys and girls? Elise says she saw a UFO last night. Can you describe it for us, Elise?"

Rosemary snickered and whispered something, and Elise wished she could take the words back. "Well, it was a bright dot. I thought it *might* be a UFO. It looked like it came down on the other side of the golf course. But Nick was looking through the binoculars."

"Two witnesses to a UFO! Isn't that fascinating! Well, Nick?" Mrs. Curley nodded past Elise. "How would you describe the UFO?"

Twisting in her seat to watch Nick, Elise was surprised to see his uninterested expression. As if he hadn't begged his grandfather to take him to where the UFO landed.

In answer to the teacher's question, Nick shrugged. "I don't know. Just a sort of bright thing. Probably a plane in trouble."

Sitting on the edge of her desk, the teacher leaned forward with her chin in her hand, eyes twinkling. "You mean it couldn't have been a UFO, Nick?"

"*UFO* just means 'unidentified flying object,'" said Nick. He didn't twinkle back at her, and he spoke as if he thought she was making a big deal out of nothing. "It doesn't mean it was an extraterrestrial spacecraft."

"Good point, Nick." The teacher's eyebrows rose approvingly, but she looked around the classroom. "Does anyone else—"

But Nick went on, "Carl Sagan thinks it would be one chance in billions that we'd ever have visitors from outer space."

15

"Good point, Nick," repeated Mrs. Curley. "Have you all seen the famous astronomer Carl Sagan on TV? Did you have something to say about that, Tim?"

Elise turned around again in surprise, but she could see by the grin on Tim's face that he wasn't thinking about the famous astronomer. "What did the thirsty Martian say to the Coke machine?"

Mrs. Curley looked annoyed. "I didn't mean you could tell a riddle, but all right, Tim. What did the thirsty Martian say to the Coke machine?"

"Take me to your *liter!*"

As giggles burst out around the room and the teacher smiled patiently, Elise glanced back at Nick. He wasn't laughing. He was staring out the window, the way Elise often did herself, as if he saw something exciting in his mind's eye. Then he caught her looking at him, and his face went blank.

At lunchtime Elise got behind Carrie and pushed her tray along the cafeteria line. Behind Elise was Tim, and then Nick, explaining to Tim what it would be like if the cafeteria were up in space, weightless. "See, in free fall everything floats around in the air currents. So that soup, if you dumped it out of the bowl, it would wobble around in a blob until it splatted on someone's hair."

Tim crowed. "Nice!" Then he added, in a different tone, "Hey, look. You're going bald."

Elise turned to stare at Nick, who must have messed up his hair showing how the soup blob would land. As thick as Husky dog fur, the hair was sticking every

which way on the top of his head. A bald spot the size of a dime showed just above his hairline, on the right.

"No, I'm not," Nick answered Tim. "That's just a little bump. See, I've got one on the other side, too. I've had them since I was a baby."

"Oh, yeah." Tim peered at his friend's scalp. "By the way—how come you rode the bus to school today?"

"Because my mom and dad went to Bermuda," answered Nick cheerfully. "I'm staying with my grandfather, and it's too far to walk. Better not open those potato chips, or they'll float away before you can eat them."

Elise put a sandwich on her tray, thinking that she liked her kind of pretending better than Nick's. When Nick imagined he was an astronaut, he had to worry about his soup wobbling off in the wrong direction. Elise's star people, with their superior technology, had solved all those problems a long time ago. Elise could just go ahead and have interesting adventures with them.

Following Carrie toward the girls' table, Elise let one of her tapes run in her head.

As the girl with the masses of tawny hair and the fierce dark eyes trudged toward the cafeteria table with her thin, flabby ham sandwich, she was suddenly aware of a quiet hum above her head. Glancing up, she saw a silver hatch open, and a ladder of silken cords and ivory rungs tumbled down.

"Child of the stars!" a clear voice rang out. "Come to us—make haste!"

18

Dropping her loathsome lunch, the girl seized the ladder and—

"Hey, Elise." Rosemary's mean, piercing voice pulled Elise's attention away from the star people. "I bet that was your space mom and dad up in the UFO last night, looking for you. Why didn't they just scoop you up? You know, with something like a pooper scooper."

There were giggles around the table. "You're the one who needs scooping, *Rosemary,*" snapped Carrie. But in a quieter tone, she asked Elise, "If it was really a UFO, wouldn't Nick be able to tell? Because he was the one with the binoculars, so . . ."

Elise felt a flash of anger at Nick. Why wouldn't he say what he had seen? Raising her voice deliberately, she answered, "I know Nick saw something, and he acted like it was something strange."

The girls turned to look at Nick, but he only scowled down at his soup bowl. "*Did* you see a UFO, no kidding?" asked Tim.

"Oh, no, no!" Rosemary's shrill voice rose over all the others. "Only Elise can see UFOs, because, you see, Elise is a child of the stars."

"*Shut up,*" said Elise.

"Elise, child of the stars!" Tim folded his ears so that they looked pointed, like Mr. Spock's in "Star Trek." "Are you a Vulcan, Elise?"

"You mean, E-*loose,*" shouted Rosemary.

There was an outbreak of giggles and exclamations. "E-loose!" "She looks like an alien to me!"

Over the chatter Elise heard Nick mutter, "This is stupid." She turned to see him chomping into his sand-

19

wich, his head bent. As if he couldn't help it, he glanced up at Elise. Then, quickly, he lowered his head again.

He did see something, thought Elise, but he won't say so. What a jerk. I knew he was conceited, but I didn't know he was mean, too.

After lunch, Mrs. Curley called Nick and Elise up to her desk. Elise was off in a daydream again, and Carrie had to poke her arm.

"Nick and Elise, would you come up here and chat with me for a moment, please?" By Mrs. Curley's tone of voice, and the fact that Nick was halfway to her desk, Elise could tell that Mrs. Curley had already said this once. "Everyone else open your science books to page 86 and read 'Our Body's Sense Organs.'"

As Elise stood up, she heard Rosemary whisper gleefully. "Uh-oh! I bet they copied from books."

Elise felt her heart flip again, as if now she were going to be punished for writing about her secret daydream. But no, Mrs. Curley wouldn't be beaming like that if she were going to accuse them of copying.

"Nick, Elise. I have an idea for the two of you that I think is going to be very exciting."

Elise looked away, wishing the teacher wouldn't make her eyes sparkle like that. She noticed that Nick was waiting with his arms folded, his eyes calm and unsmiling. Just spit it out, Mrs. Curley, he seemed to be thinking.

"You both wrote such outstanding papers for 'I've Got a Secret,'" the teacher went on. "Nick, you must be a chip off the old block—your father used to be a pilot, didn't he?"

"Yes," said Nick matter-of-factly, "but of course I couldn't be a chip off the old block. I'm adopted."

"Well, of course—I meant—" The teacher looked embarrassed. She went on quickly, "Not only did you both write outstanding papers, but you both showed such a strong interest in space. And you both chose astronomy for your science enrichment projects. So I said to myself, What if these two talented heads got together?"

Elise frowned as it struck her what the teacher was getting at. It must have struck Nick at the same time, because he frowned, too, and took a step backward.

"You'd be a winning team!" Mrs. Curley smiled even more, giving them a little wink.

Elise felt about the way she would have if Mrs. Curley had said, "I think you and Nick should get married!" She struggled to think of an excuse.

"I've already done half of my project *by myself*," said Nick in a politely sorry tone. "On meteors."

"Yeah, me, too!" Elise chimed in breathlessly. "I mean, I'm doing mine on UFOs."

"Now, I know your approaches to the subject of space are different," said Mrs. Curley, still smiling, as if Nick and Elise had liked her idea, "but that's exactly why you have a lot to learn from each other."

"I'm not going to learn anything from made-up stuff about UFOs," said Nick. He seemed to become more solid as he stood there, like concrete hardening. "I thought this was supposed to be a *science* report."

21

"See?" said Elise. She brushed her springy hair back from her face. "UFOs won't appear to people who don't believe in them. He'd ruin my project."

Mrs. Curley was leaning across her desk, looking from Nick to Elise. She spoke in a low, intense voice. "The most important thing you can learn in school is to work with different kinds of people." She wasn't beaming anymore. "I think if you two could cooperate to pool Elise's splendid imagination and Nick's keen intellect, you'd come up with something very special. You could start by investigating the area where that UFO seemed to land last night."

Elise squirmed. How could Mrs. Curley think this was such a good idea when it was such a bad idea? "I'm supposed to practice tennis this afternoon."

"Yeah, and anyway, where would we look?" asked Nick reasonably. "I couldn't follow the thing with the binoculars, so we wouldn't know where to go. Anyway, this doesn't have anything to do with my project on meteors."

He's lying, thought Elise. I told him it disappeared over near his house. He tried to get his grandfather to take him over there.

"You know, I'm a little disappointed." Mrs. Curley looked reproachfully from one to the other. "I thought the two of you would jump at the chance to do some original research. The other side of the golf course is close enough for both of you to walk, and it's a nice sunny day."

"I have to practice tennis this afternoon," said Elise.

Nick gave the teacher a brisk smile. "I guess it's not

going to work out. Interesting idea, though, Mrs. Curley."

Elise smiled, too, as she edged away from the teacher's desk. To herself she said, No, Mrs. Curley, I wouldn't jump at the chance to do more research. Elise had one more book, *Pharaohs and UFOs,* to look at, and that was going to be the end of her science enrichment project.

Back in her seat, Elise heard Nick telling Tim about Mrs. Curley's crazy idea. Carrie was listening, too, rolling her eyes at Elise and snickering with her hand over her mouth. Elise gave Carrie a little push, but she couldn't help smiling, herself.

She didn't want to do a research project with Nick, but she *would* like to know why he was acting so strange.

A Winning Team

Getting off the school bus later that afternoon, Elise was looking forward to a snack and some time to herself. But as she came into the kitchen, her mother stopped talking on the phone and fixed her with an intent stare. "Honey, I want you to let me make an appointment to get your hair cut this week. It's out of control."

"No!" Elise put her hands to her head as if her mother were coming at her with the scissors. "You *promised* I didn't have to get it cut if I brushed it myself."

"You're sure you brushed that?" asked Mrs. Hall doubtfully. "It looks so wild."

"Yes! Just because it doesn't look like yours—" Mom's straight hair was cut so that it fell neatly into place, even after she had played three sets of tennis.

Mrs. Hall spoke into the phone. "Can I call you right back, Terry?" She pushed up the sleeves of her pink sweat suit as she turned to Elise. "I've got to work out a few things about the Boosters' rummage sale, so why don't you go on up to the tennis courts and practice on the backboard until I get there." She nodded toward Elise's racket and a tote bag of tennis balls, standing by the door.

"Practice tennis?" Elise had hoped her mother would forget about that.

"Yes, remember, we talked this morning about how they just put up the nets last weekend?" Her mother smiled. "I love the spring! It's so neat to get back to outdoor tennis. But what I'm saying about your hair, honey, is I don't think you realize how much prettier it would be if it weren't so—so wild. For heaven's sake, don't give me that look." Mrs. Hall gave a little laugh and patted the sides of Elise's wiry mop. "I'm not trying to make you cut your hair *short.* Just a medium-length cut, with a little shaping, would make a world of difference."

Pulling her head away, Elise picked up the racket and balls without answering and stalked out the back door. Of course getting her hair cut would make a world of difference. That's why Elise wouldn't do it.

She dragged her feet along the road, kicking gravel. Why couldn't Mom leave her alone? Mom and Dad and Lewis liked tennis. Elise didn't; she had tried tennis lessons last summer.

"If you'd just pay attention, Elise, you'd make some progress and then you'd get to like it," her mother had said. "Heads up, Elise!" Cathy, the tennis instructor, had called, over and over. "Pay attention!"

That was when the daydream about the star people had first come to Elise—during a tennis lesson. She had popped the ball up over the fence, and had to go in back of the courts to look for it. *As the girl poked around in the poison ivy with her tennis racket, she caught her first glimpse of the silvery starship glinting through the underbrush. She heard the star woman exclaim, "At last, we have found her! The tawny-haired one who is to save our world from certain doom."*

Strolling down the road past Mr. Russell's little house with the blue Honda in the driveway, up the path through the pines, Elise began to swing her racket cheerfully. She wished she'd grabbed some crackers on her way out, but she was glad to be outdoors. It was a fresh, damp April afternoon, with the sun glinting off the pine needles.

When she reached the tennis courts beside the golf course, Elise's spirits rose another notch. An older girl was already pounding away at the backboard, so Elise wouldn't have to start practicing until her mother showed up.

Sitting on the rail fence outside the courts, Elise shut her eyes against the bright sunlight and felt the breeze lift her hair. She began to run the tape in her head again.

With an amused smile, the star woman took the tennis racket from Elise's hand and dropped it down the recycling chute. At the same time, the star man stepped forward with a sword laid across his palms.

The sword was small, but its blade flashed like a mirror, dazzling Elise. The star man spoke. "Know that it is you, and only you, who can save our world from direst peril."

Pounding footsteps broke into the daydream, and Elise blinked and squinted into the sunlight. For a second she didn't recognize the boy running up the road to the tennis courts. Since the sun had been shining on her eyelids, everything looked washed out. The boy appeared light gray, the color (some people said) of alien beings from UFOs.

But more than that, Elise had never seen such an excited expression on this boy's face before. Nick, usually so calm, was panting loudly. His eyes shone like the eyes of someone who has just won the lottery.

"What's going on?" Elise jumped down from the fence.

For a second she thought Nick was going to run on by her. Then his eyes seemed to focus on her, and he came to a halt beside the fence.

"What's the matter?" asked Elise, a little nervous at the wild look in his eyes.

"Guess I could tell you," he began, but he choked on the words. He had to lean on the fence, coughing and struggling for breath.

Elise was beginning to think she should go in the tennis office and get some help when Nick finally gasped out a few more words. "My house. In the pool!"

This sounded like something gruesome that Elise didn't want to hear about. "What? *What's* in the pool?"

Nick didn't answer right away. He raised his head and narrowed his eyes at Elise, as if he was deciding whether he could trust her or not. Then, suddenly, he said, "I'll show you. Come on."

Hesitating, Elise thought of her mother. Mom would show up at the tennis courts pretty soon, and she would expect Elise to be there. Well, actually it might be a while before Mom showed up, since she was going to talk to someone on the phone first. Mom never had any short phone conversations.

"I can't stay very long," said Elise as they started down the road. "But what *is* it?"

Nick shook his head, smiling, still breathing hard. He wouldn't say anything until they had crossed the street that divided the golf course in half. After they were on the cart path, near the marsh, he turned to Elise with an expression of triumph. "*It* is only—the most important discovery in the history of the world!"

At first Elise just stared at him, afraid he had gone crazy. Then she connected what he had said with what they had seen last night. "Oh! You mean it *was* a meteorite? There's a crater in your pool?"

Nick grinned and shook his head again. "I thought you were supposed to have such a great imagination. Come on." He began to trot toward the far edge of the golf course. "Good thing I ran into you," he added over his shoulder. "I was going to get my grandfather, but now I don't think that's such a good idea. He'd probably call the police."

"The police?" Elise was starting to think she had made a mistake in coming with him, and she stopped

28

on the path. They had reached the tall pine trees bordering the golf course. The mention of the police reminded Elise that she had left her racket, the way her mother always told her not to do, leaning against the fence, where anyone could take it. "Did someone break into your house?"

Nick looked at her with surprise, and then a smile twitched his mouth. "I think so. In a way. But you have to see. . . . Come on, my yard's right through there."

Following him under the pines, Elise saw a row of evergreen shrubs, and then a stretch of lawn, and then the back of a two-story house with a big deck. In the middle of the lawn was a swimming pool, a plastic cover stretched over it. Instead of sagging in the middle, the cover bulged up.

Before he stepped onto the lawn, Nick gave Elise a gleeful glance, as if he was ready to hear applause. Then he marched to the swimming pool, stooped down, and lifted the edge of the cover. "Look."

Elise had been so nervous she would see something horrible, like a dead animal, that for a moment she couldn't understand what she was looking at. It was a dark, curved surface of some glossy material. Gingerly she put her fingertips on it. It was hard, and so smooth that it felt almost oily. But when she took her hand away, there was nothing on her fingers. She looked at Nick, baffled. "What is it?"

He frowned. "Can't you guess now? Get down and look under, so you can see the whole thing."

More puzzled than ever, Elise crouched on the grass

and stuck her head right under the cover, while Nick held it up. She drew in her breath.

In the dim light under the plastic cover, she could see that the dark, glossy thing almost filled the swimming pool. It was the shape of two Frisbees glued together, bulging out at the top and bottom.

Pulling her head out, Elise stared at Nick. "*What is it?* Just tell me. What do you *think* it is?"

Nick glanced over her head in the direction of the house. "I can't believe you. It was your idea in the first place." He let the cover drop back over the edge of the pool as he went on in a low voice. "Okay. You know the thing you saw last night? You thought it was a UFO. Well, I knew it was. I saw it."

"But you wouldn't say— You told Mrs.—" Elise sputtered. She knew he had been hiding something.

"I wasn't going to tell *her* anything," said Nick impatiently. "Anyway—" He paused and took a deep breath, his eyes shining. "This has to be it."

Elise pulled up the cover again, just far enough to see the deep gleam of the whatever-it-was. "But the thing in the sky was bright."

Nick shrugged. "They could have had the lights on."

"They?" Elise's heart began to thud. She pushed herself up and backed away from the pool. "Who's *they?*"

"What's the matter with you?" said Nick sharply. "You're the one who wrote all that stuff about star people. *I* thought it was a bunch of baloney. But now here this is, and you're acting stupid."

Elise stood up straight and folded her arms. "Okay,

if you're so smart, where are they? Are they"—she pointed to the swimming pool cover—"inside?"

Nick shook his head and looked across the lawn toward the blank windows of the house. "I'm not sure, but . . . I think I saw someone moving in there."

At that Elise felt cold inside. "We have to tell the police!" she blurted out, and she backed toward the shelter of the trees.

"Wait!" Grabbing her arm, Nick still spoke in a low tone, as if someone nearby might hear him. "No. Don't get the police. They might not handle this right. And it might get all mixed up, so that everyone forgets I discovered the—" He nodded toward the swimming pool cover.

"What do you want to do, then?" Elise stared at him, exasperated. She had always thought of Nick as a boy who was more sensible than a normal kid ought to be, but now he seemed to have gone too far in the other direction.

Nick squinted thoughtfully. "I think the obvious thing to do is call Carl Sagan. He's in Cambridge this year, so he could get here pretty quickly."

Impatiently Elise huffed her breath out. "How do you know—this might not be what you think at all. That thing in the pool might be a—a weird work of art, like my cousin in New York makes. Did you go look in your house to see if there were really . . . star people?"

"That might be dangerous," said Nick in his normal sensible voice. "How do I know they're friendly?"

"How do you know they're star people?" asked Elise

mockingly. She was more and more sure that Nick had jumped to the wrong conclusion. "I bet you're scared to go in there. I dare you."

Nick scowled at her. "I can't go in because I'd have to get the key from my grandfather. If you're so brave, why don't you go look in the window?"

Elise was a little sorry she had started this, but she answered, "I will if you will."

Without any more talking, Elise and Nick marched across the lawn to the deck. As she climbed the steps ahead of Nick, though, Elise's marching turned into sneaking. Her heart started tripping, and she remembered all her parents' warnings about kidnappers. She also remembered a dream she'd had last week, about running in slow motion while a kidnapper's swift footsteps thudded behind her.

Elise and Nick crept across the deck, the boards creaking. The view inside the sliding glass door was blocked by drapes, but at the far end of the deck there was a greenhouse window.

Reaching the window first, Elise sidled up to the edge of it until she could peek through the geraniums into the kitchen.

Then Elise's joints went all loose. Her heart seemed to leap into her throat.

There were two of them. Lying right there on the kitchen counters. The one propped on his elbows turned his head and looked straight at her. Then he sat up and touched the things on his head to the things on the other's head and pointed at Elise.

With a strangled squawk, Elise whirled and charged

blindly into Nick, making him stumble against the railing. But she plunged onward, flying off the deck without touching the three steps, scrambling across the lawn without a glance over her shoulder to see whose footsteps were gaining on her.

Child of the Stars

As Elise ran, a kind of prayer babbled inside her head: Please, no, I didn't mean it, I'll never wish that again, no, please. . . . In a flash she understood a thing she had never thought of before. She understood what it would *really* be like to be picked up and taken off by star people. It would mean no more pleasant walks to the golf course and the tennis courts, no more afternoons fooling around with Carrie, no more butterscotch pudding or fried chicken, no more—

"Stop running!" shouted Nick, almost in her ear.

Elise was already crashing through the evergreen shrubs, but she let the branches slow her down and looked over her shoulder. The lawn was empty, except for the swimming pool.

"Nobody's coming after us," Nick went on as he stooped behind the bushes. "And nobody can see us here." He stared at her curiously. "Well, what did you see?"

Elise stooped beside him on shaky knees. "There were two of them," she gasped. She caught her breath, then added in a low voice, "They had antennas."

Nick looked puzzled. "Antennas? You mean like space suits with radio antennas?"

"No." Elise shuddered. "Antennas coming out of their hair. Like bugs." She put her hands on top of her head, her forefingers curled out like feelers.

"You mean antenn*ae,* then," Nick corrected her, pronouncing *antennae* to rhyme with *penny.* "So they looked like bugs?"

"No," said Elise, frustrated. This was as hard as making someone else understand what a dream had been like. It was all so clear to her, especially her feeling that she would never get away no matter how fast she ran. "Like men wearing long underwear. Orange. Only they had antennas. Antennae."

"Orange long underwear?" Nick frowned. "What were they doing?"

"Lying there," said Elise. Then she remembered an open cracker box and a tube in one star man's hands. Slowly she added, "They were eating crackers with—with toothpaste on them."

Nick gave her a look of disbelief. "I knew I should have gone first. Toothpaste! It must have been a tube of cheese spread."

"It wasn't," said Elise, although now she wondered. The tube was red and white with white letters, just like the kind of toothpaste the Halls used, and the stuff squeezing out onto the cracker was white. But some kinds of cheese were white. And maybe she just thought she had read the letters on the tube.

"Actually," Nick was saying thoughtfully, "maybe they are eating toothpaste. If they're lying around with antennae on their heads, they must be crazy." A look of great disappointment, as if he had lost a million dollars, came over his face. "And that thing in the swimming pool. I don't know *what* they're trying to do." Rising to his feet, he brushed the pine needles off his jeans. "I guess I'd better go tell Grandpa."

"Just a minute," said Elise. She crawled to the shelter of the trees before she stood up. "You're talking like they're people. Well, they aren't. I'm not sure about the toothpaste, but I *saw* their antennas."

"Antenn*ae,*" said Nick absently, already halfway through the pine trees. "Come *on.* Anybody can buy those antenna headbands at Woolworth's. But they really fooled me with the model spaceship. I wonder if they did the UFO with some kind of special effects, too. Maybe the whole thing is like publicity for a movie."

Elise hurried to catch up with him. "You've got the wrong idea! Their antennae weren't headbands from Woolworth's. They looked more like asparagus, and I saw them moving, not just bouncing around like those fake ones." She could tell he wasn't listening; Nick had already made up his mind that Elise didn't know the difference between what she imagined and what was real.

Following Nick out of the trees, onto the rough grass between the golf course fairway and the marsh, Elise tried again. She said something she had been thinking but was afraid to say out loud. "Maybe that's how they found me—with their antennae."

Shaking his head, Nick gave her a scornful smile. "Save it for Mrs. Curley. She likes that made-up stuff. If aliens were looking for you with their special powers and all that junk, why would they go to *my* house? Their wonderful antennae must not work that well."

"Oh." Elise felt stupid, but at the same time the sick feeling in her stomach faded a little. That was a good question—why *had* they gone to Nick's house? "I thought maybe they could pick up what I was thinking. I thought maybe"—this was sounding stupider and stupider, now that she said it out loud—"maybe when I made up that story about how I was really a star person, that was like sending them a message. Maybe."

Nick's only answer to this was a snort. They walked on without speaking for a while, past the marsh and up a hill to the ninth green. The breeze Elise had felt by the tennis courts had turned into a brisk wind, blowing in her face and bending and rattling last year's rushes in the marsh.

By this time, Elise wasn't sure what she had seen. Well, she *had* seen two people—men, she thought—wearing what looked like fur hats and rust-colored long underwear. They were lying on the kitchen counters and spreading something on crackers. And they had two things on their heads. But was she so sure they weren't antenna headbands? Maybe she had listened to the tapes she ran in her head so long that she *was* losing track of what was real and what was made up. But if she had, it was Nick's fault, too, with all his mysterious talk about "them."

Trying to get over feeling foolish, Elise ran up the hill ahead of Nick. As she waited for him at the top, she noticed that he didn't *look* as if he was going to make fun of her and tell all the kids at school what a space shot she was. Nick's eyes had a thoughtful squint, as if he had been trying to figure something out. "What I don't get," he said, "is how they could have put together such a realistic spaceship. It must be for a movie set. I've never seen anything like that."

"How could they be making a movie in your back-yard?" said Elise. "They'd have to ask your folks. It looked more like one of those big weird pieces of art. Like my cousin Patty in New York makes. They're so big you can walk through them, and they look like they came from outer space."

"That doesn't make sense either," said Nick. "Why would anyone build a— Hey, there's a lady waving at us."

"Uh-oh," said Elise, turning from Nick to look across the street. Standing on the road that led to the tennis courts' parking lot, holding *two* tennis rackets, was a woman in a pink sweat suit. "My mom. She didn't talk on the phone as long as I thought. Now I'm going to get it."

The next morning, as Mrs. Curley was writing a list of words to alphabetize on the board, Elise told Carrie about her mother wanting Elise to have her hair cut.

40

"My mom's much worse," whispered Carrie, whose hair had finally grown back over her ears in the last couple of weeks. She imitated her mother's sharp voice. "Just jump in the car, young lady. Do you know how many girls would *love* the chance to go to the hairdresser, only their families can't afford it?"

Elise smothered a laugh. "Well, how many?"

"I never found out," said Carrie with a grin.

Mrs. Curley glanced over her shoulder, tapping the chalk on the board. "While I'm writing this list, boys and girls, you're copying it down. Your eyes are on the board or on your papers, and your mouths are shut."

Elise and Carrie shut their mouths, but behind them Nick was still whispering with Tim. "Why do you keep scratching your head?" Tim was asking in a tone of pretended politeness. "Fleas?"

"I'm scratching because it itches, dum-dum," Nick answered. "Maybe I've got poison ivy."

"Poison ivy? Hey, do you know what would happen if you walked through a patch of poison ivy holding a rabbit's foot?" Giggling, Tim didn't wait for an answer. "You'd have a rash of good luck!"

Nick laughed a little, but he only said, "Do you want to hear about the police or not?"

"Okay, okay. So you told your grandfather, and he called the police."

"Yeah," said Nick, "but I guess they didn't turn on their sirens or anything like that. They just drove over and met my grandfather at our house—he wouldn't let me come along—and checked inside. But the men were gone. They must have run away when they heard the cars drive up. And nothing was missing."

41

Tim snickered softly. "Except toothpaste. Those guys just came in, put on their antenna headbands, and ate some toothpaste on crackers. Then they said, 'I'm outa here.'"

"It's not that funny," said Nick. "If these weird guys showed up at your house—"

"—they'd fit right in!"

Elise's pencil copied the words from the board, but she was wondering, What about the spaceship?

She didn't have a chance to ask Nick anything until time for computer practice. As she and Nick and the other kids in their computer group walked down the hall to the library, she hurried to catch up with him. "When the police went to your house, did they look in the swimming pool?"

Nick shook his head as he kept on rubbing it with one hand. "I didn't tell my grandfather about the pool. I didn't want them to look there because I was hoping the weirdos would run away and leave the mock-up." His eyes shone. "That'd be such a cool thing to have."

Elise remembered the solid, slippery feel of the dark surface, and she felt uneasy. "I think the police should have looked at it."

Usually, sitting in front of a computer screen with no one watching her made a daydream tape start running in Elise's head. But today what came to her was not a daydream, but something upsettingly real. The words and picture on the screen seemed to fade away, replaced by scenes that fit together like steps in a computer program:

Nick reminding Mrs. Curley, "I'm adopted."

42

Nick saying to Elise, "If aliens were looking for you with their special powers and all that junk, why would they go to *my* house?"

Nick telling Tim yesterday about the two bumps on his head, "I've had them since I was a baby."

Nick scratching his head because the spots itched, because . . .

"Oh!" groaned Elise, looking over at Nick. The sick, nightmarish feeling of yesterday afternoon gripped her again.

Nick, bent over his keyboard, didn't even notice. But the library aide stepped to Elise's side. "Come on, it's not the end of the world if you make a mistake. Just press 'Escape,' or— Now wait a minute. You're making a fuss over nothing. This is *right*, Elise!" The woman smiled at her encouragingly. "I bet you can figure out the next step."

But Elise couldn't. How do you tell a boy like Nick that he's really a child of the stars?

Adopted by Earthlings

Elise made herself work at the program until the library aide went away. But then she just sat there with her awful feeling, staring at the screen. When she thought the star people had come to get *her*, it was as if a door, the door to the whole world, had shut in her face. And Mom and Dad and Carrie and Mrs. Curley and the kids at school and Elise's cozy bedroom and summer vacation at the beach and Christmas and—*everything* were all on the other side.

Elise didn't want to be the one to make Nick feel like that. On the other hand, she ought to warn him. He ought to have a chance to hide or tell his grandfather or call up his parents in Bermuda.

But Elise couldn't talk to Nick during computer practice, and the aide kept her for a few minutes after the other kids left, trying to explain something. Elise couldn't pay attention to anything right now except what she was going to do about Nick, but she had to sit and pretend to listen.

Later, when the fifth graders went to lunch, Elise walked toward the cafeteria right behind Nick. She watched him scratching the top of his head, first one spot and then the other. Now, she thought. Tell him.

But she didn't. Again, at recess, when the fifth graders played kickball, Elise found herself waiting beside Nick for a turn at the plate. It was starting to drizzle—heavy mist, really. She kept glancing sideways at the droplets caught in Nick's thick, furlike hair, and she wondered why no one had guessed the truth about him before.

Still she couldn't make herself say anything. It's not the kind of thing you can tell someone to his face, she decided. I'll write him a note.

After lunch, most of the class worked on metric problems while Ms. Wasserman, the remedial math teacher, taught a small group. Elise saw her chance when Ms. Wasserman started to leave and Mrs. Curley walked toward the door, chatting with her.

Mrs. Curley didn't notice Elise taking out a sheet of lined paper, but Carrie did. She leaned over curiously. "What's that for?"

"This is private," said Elise, shielding the paper with her left shoulder as she wrote:

Nick:

Don't feel bad, but I think you're a star person adopted by Earth people. And that's why they came to your house.

46

You can hide at my house if you want.

Elise

Of course Nick probably wouldn't be any safer at her house than at his grandfather's, but Elise felt so bad for him, she had to offer to help in some way. With her mind's eye she saw the dark, glossy Frisbee of the spaceship gliding over the tops of the pine trees, searching, searching. Inside the ship, the star men twitched their antennae like the noses of dogs tracking a rabbit.

Folding the note and folding it again to make sure no one could peek inside, Elise wrote "Nick" on the outside. *"Oh,"* said Carrie in a meaningful tone.

But Elise ignored that. Glancing toward the teacher, she saw that Mrs. Curley was in the doorway, still talking to Ms. Wasserman. Good. Elise turned around and held the folded note out to Nick.

Nick looked at it with a puzzled frown, as if it couldn't be for him. "Here," whispered Elise, sliding the note across his desk.

Nick finally put out his hand, but Tim's hand was much quicker. "And there's an intercept by Perillo!" he said in a voice like a sports announcer.

"Hey!" Elise grabbed, but Tim already had the note spread open under his desk.

"Woo, woo!" Tim rolled his eyes. "Listen to this, folks. 'You can hide at my house. Love, Elise.'"

"Sh!" Fearfully Elise looked around for the teacher, but Mrs. Curley had strolled out into the hall with Ms. Wasserman. "It doesn't say 'love,'" she hissed. To her horror, all the kids around them seemed to be listening. One boy sidled over, keeping an eye on the door, to get a look at the note.

"It's just dumb stuff," Nick told them all. Yanking the note from Tim's hand, he crumpled it into his pocket.

Carrie whispered to Elise, "I *thought* you must like Nick."

"I don't!" Elise was just thinking that the worst possible thing had happened to the note, when she noticed the boy who had been out of his seat scooting back into it.

Tim, glancing over her shoulder, said, "You're in deep marshmallow." Elise turned to see Mrs. Curley standing beside them.

"Give me the note, please, Nick," said the teacher. To the whole class she added, "You know that I think letters are wonderful. They're such a good way to express yourself and practice communication skills. I wish you would all write more letters. There's only one kind of letter writing I don't like. Do you know what kind that is, Elise?"

"Passing notes in class," muttered Elise. Now her best hope was that Mrs. Curley would throw the note away.

But the teacher was smoothing out the crumpled paper. As she ran her eyes over it, she frowned. "I just don't understand you, Elise and Nick. If you're playing games like this, why wouldn't you take my suggestion to work on a project together?"

"I don't understand either," said Rosemary in a low, gushy tone, "because they're in *love.*"

48

Mrs. Curley's frown deepened in Rosemary's direction, but she didn't say anything more about what was in the note. "Elise, you may stand in the hall until time for dismissal."

Out in the hall, Elise had a good long time to gaze at the cutouts of spring flowers taped on the walls and to think about what had gone wrong. In the first place, why, why, *why* hadn't Nick taken her note before Tim grabbed it? Had Nick read it before he put it in his pocket? If he hadn't, Elise would still have to tell him.

On the other hand, why hadn't Elise talked to Nick instead of writing a note? She had had enough chances to talk to him.

Elise wished there were something to do out here besides worry. She was bored but too nervous to daydream. She leaned her back against the wall, braced her feet, and let herself slide down until she was sitting on the floor. She *had* to make sure that Nick knew. Maybe she could say something to him when they got on the bus.

Finally it was three o'clock, and Elise came into the classroom to line up with the others. She heard Tim, ahead of her in line, ask Nick, "Were you playing some kind of game with her about aliens? Like, the burglars at your house were really star people?"

"The note was just stupid fooling around." Nick's voice was strained. He put his hand up to his head as if he were going to scratch it, but then he took it away. "I don't know why she wrote me a note."

"I think she *likes* you." Tim snickered. "Do you like her?"

At that, Elise glanced uneasily at Nick, expecting him to say something really horrible about her. But Nick didn't seem to be paying attention to what Tim might be thinking about him and Elise. There was a faraway look on his face. "Stupid," he repeated, but without much energy.

Outside the front of the school, as she climbed into her bus, Elise noticed Nick going off with the other kids who walked to school. But he was supposed to ride her bus. He had been riding it all this week because he was staying with his grandfather.

Then he must not be going to his grandfather's.

Elise froze at the front of the bus, watching through the drizzle on the windshield as Nick turned the corner onto Mallard Street. Mallard was the street that divided the golf course in half. Nick was going to walk up to the golf course, along the edge of the marsh to the pine trees—and through the trees to his house.

Nick couldn't go back to his house by himself! What if *they* were still there?

"Excuse me," said Elise breathlessly, trying to push her way down the bus steps. Nick must be going there on purpose to meet them. But why? It was just the opposite of what Elise would have done. Maybe she shouldn't have told him.

"You're going the wrong way, Toots," barked the bus driver, a woman with a leathery face. "Move to the back of the bus and sit down."

On the other hand, thought Elise, turning around and letting herself be pushed toward the back of the bus, what could I do if I did run after Nick? I couldn't

stop him. And besides, maybe the star people are gone for good. Probably they are.

As Elise pushed open the wooden gate of her yard, she noticed that her mother's Jeep was missing from the driveway. Mom was probably at a rummage sale meeting. Pausing in the kitchen doorway, Elise heard loud talking, over loud music on a sound track, coming from the family room. That room was full of Lewis and his friends, watching a movie. If Mom were around, she'd make them turn down the volume—in fact, she wouldn't let Lewis watch this movie, judging from the comments the boys were shouting.

Elise unzipped her jacket, but she didn't take it off. Maybe she should have jumped off the bus and run after Nick. Maybe she should walk over to his house now to make sure he was all right.

No. She couldn't do that. Elise's stomach quivered with fear. She couldn't go back to that house, with those people—who weren't even human beings—inside.

Elise felt ashamed. Chicken! she called herself. I thought you were the tawny-haired one who could save a whole world from certain doom.

Still, instead of going after Nick, she decided to call his grandfather.

When Elise dialed Mr. Russell's number, there was no answer. What now? Elise wondered, hanging up. As she hesitated, her jacket still on, the phone rang.

Carrie's eager voice spoke in her ear. "Hi! Did Nick say anything to you on the bus? Did he sit with you?"

"No," said Elise slowly. She didn't want to explain to Carrie that Nick wasn't on the bus at all, or why.

"Well, don't worry, he's probably just a little shy. The kids on my bus were talking about it"—Elise's face went hot—"and we think maybe he likes you anyway because when you had to stand in the hall, he looked like he thought Mrs. Curley was being mean."

Elise snorted. "How could you tell what he was thinking?"

"I can tell," said Carrie. "Like there's this boy Judd who goes to my church, and I thought for a long time he was looking at me funny, and sure enough, he gave me a valentine."

"Yeah, you showed it to me," said Elise. It hadn't been much of a valentine—just one of the flimsy kind you buy in a big package, twenty little valentines without envelopes for $1.98. Carrie's had a picture of a carrot with a smiling face and a throbbing heart, and it said, "Valentine! Do you *carrot* all for me?"

But Carrie wanted to tell Elise the whole story about Judd, all over again, from the first sideways glances during Christmas caroling to the day he actually handed her the valentine with the smiling carrot.

Finally Elise told Carrie she had to do her homework, and she hung up. She did have to do her homework. But when she had spread the contents of her book bag over her bed and started working the multiplication problems, her mind drifted off.

Why had Nick acted like such an idiot, hurrying to meet the aliens at his house? What if they grabbed him and took off for the stars again? Wasn't he worried about that? If *she* were Nick, she'd never—

Just a minute, thought Elise, biting her pencil in surprise. If I were Nick, I'd be adopted. I'd wonder what

53

my real parents were like. If I thought I could see them . . .

Elise should have thought of that before, that the star people in Nick's house might be his parents. She had thought they were both men, but maybe just because of their short hair. Remembering their blank faces with the twitching asparagus feelers above, she felt very sorry for Nick. Imagine calling those weird people Mom and Dad!

The real trouble, though, was that Nick's star parents must have come to take him back. Elise should tell Mr. Russell. Tell him *something*, so it wouldn't be her fault.

Going downstairs to the kitchen, Elise stood in front of the phone. Before she dialed, she tried some practice lines in her head. Mr. Russell? This is Elise. I thought you might like to know . . .

That was where it got difficult.

I thought you might like to know that Nick is really an alien.

I thought you might like to know that the UFO we saw was Nick's real parents.

I thought—

Lewis swaggered into the kitchen, interrupting her thoughts. "Heh-wo," he lisped mockingly, taking a can of soda from the refrigerator. "Having twouble using the tewephone?"

That did it. Elise clenched her teeth and started to punch Mr. Russell's number into the phone. But before she finished, the kitchen door opened.

"Hi, honey," said her mother, hanging her raincoat on the rack by the door.

Elise hung up the phone and turned meaningfully toward Lewis, hoping he would get in trouble for the movie he and his friends were watching. But Lewis had already disappeared into the family room. Instead of the heavy beat of rock music, there was suddenly the earnest conversation from an After School Special.

"Nick Russell looks like he'd be a good athlete," remarked Mrs. Hall. "Does he play tennis?"

"Nick?" Elise caught her breath. "Did you see him outside?"

Her mother, stowing a bottle of milk in the refrigerator, gave her a surprised glance. "Yes, I saw him going into his grandfather's house. Since he's staying there for a while, wouldn't you like to practice tennis with him?"

Letting out a long sigh, Elise answered in a weak voice. "Oh. Sure." So Nick had come back safely.

For a moment Elise only felt relief, but then she started itching with curiosity. Were they there? she wanted to ask him. Did you see your real mom and dad?

The trouble was, of course, Nick and the star people couldn't talk to each other. Unless they had some kind of high-tech translating machine.

Still, they must have been able to get some things across, using gestures. For instance, Nick probably showed them the bumps on his head. What did they do then? her questions went on. And do they want you to go back with them?

That last question was the one Elise wanted answered most of all.

Don't Tell Anyone

The next morning, just as the school bus pulled up in front of Twin Ponds Lane, Nick joined the group of children waiting in the rain. "Hi," said Elise in a low tone. "Did you see your real parents?"

Nick shook his head. "But I've got to talk to you," he said as he followed her up the steps. Elise was about to whisper, "Okay, when we get to school," when she realized that Nick was sitting down beside her.

Embarrassed, Elise pushed back the hood of her slicker and glanced around to see who was watching. Boys didn't sit with girls! "What are you doing?" she whispered.

Elise knew what Carrie would have thought, but Nick didn't look at all like he was falling in love with her. The expression on his face was serious and businesslike. "Look, you have to promise to keep your mouth shut about this."

"I didn't tell anybody," said Elise. "But if they aren't your mom and dad—"

"Good. Don't tell Carrie or anyone. Pretend it was a joke. See, if a lot of people know they're here, the Patrol might find out."

"But who *are* 'they'?" Elise felt confused, trying to adjust her imaginary picture of Nick meeting his star parents. "And what's the Patrol?"

"The Patrol . . ." Nick shut his eyes, as if trying to translate a word from a foreign language. "I guess I said that because I got the impression they were like the highway patrol, only they're watching starships. One thing I know is that they try to stop anyone from visiting the Earth."

"They must be like guardians of the galaxy!" exclaimed Elise, trying to keep her voice low. "They watch over younger planets like us and keep them from doing stupid things, like killing all the whales."

Nick raised one eyebrow at her. "Cut that out. I don't know *what* the Patrol is, except the Thubans at my house—"

"Thubans?" interrupted Elise.

"Thuban is the star they're from. But the main thing is, they could get in big trouble with this Patrol. They can't stay any longer than sundown tomorrow, and if they're worried, they might leave before that."

"Go ahead!" said a gleeful voice above them. "Kiss!"

Elise looked up from their whispering to see the

grinning face of another boy, leaning over the back of the seat in front of them. In fact, kids all around them were leaning toward Nick and Elise, looking as if they expected some fun.

"Oh, brother," muttered Nick in disgust. He pushed himself out of the seat, swinging his book bag at the head of the other boy. "Just don't tell anyone *anything*," he commanded Elise once more.

"*In* your seat while the bus is moving!" barked the driver at Nick. But he was already sliding down beside another boy, two rows back.

"Tell us," crooned the boy leaning over the seat to Elise. "Tell us how much he loves you."

Elise paid no attention. Nick had talked to the star people! But they weren't the star people Elise had imagined for Nick—they weren't his parents.

Why *hadn't* his parents come to get him? And what were these two Thubans doing, sneaking around and hiding from a Patrol?

Elise jounced along on the noisy school bus, smelling the damp clothes and vinyl raincoats and tingling with excitement. This was not a daydream.

Elise had a lot more questions for Nick, but she didn't get to ask any after they got to school. In the classroom Tim started trading riddles with him right away. After lunch, the rain had stopped and Nick got into a soccer game, so Elise gave up and joined Carrie and some other girls for jacks.

Between her turns at jacks—which were very short, since she wasn't paying attention and never got beyond twosies—Elise thought about the little Nick had told her.

He hadn't said *how* the aliens in the Patrol could find out about other aliens visiting the Earth, but Elise had an idea. One of her research books on UFOs had said that TV signals went far out into space, where beings from other planets could pick them up. If the news got out that there was a UFO in Rushfield, and if the Patrol happened to watch that story on the news, they would know.

Aliens watching Earth TV! What did they think? Elise imagined state troopers with feelers on their heads. Lounging in their starship as it glided around the globe, they would take notes on "Wheel of Fortune" and "Sesame Street" and MTV.

As they were walking back to the classroom, Carrie asked Elise, "Want to come over after school? We can walk down to the Post Road Tavern and see if they'll give us free water and popcorn."

Elise hesitated. "Yeah, it would be fun, but I guess I can't. I have to do something else."

Carrie frowned, then smiled knowingly. "Oh. With Nick."

"It's not that!" said Elise. "I mean, I have to talk to him, but it's not—"

"Is that why you kept looking at him when we were playing jacks?" asked Carrie. "I *wondered* why you never got any further than twosies." It didn't matter how Elise explained it—Carrie had made up her mind there was a romance going on.

As it happened, Elise got a chance to talk to Nick

before school was out. She had forgotten about their clarinet lesson and the fact that just the two of them would be walking together from their classroom to the cafeteria. Nick must have forgotten, too, because he looked at Elise uneasily as she fell into step with him.

"So how did you know they weren't your parents?" she started right in.

Nick frowned straight ahead, swinging his instrument case. "I can't tell you any more. It might ruin everything for me."

"If you don't want me to tell anyone else," snapped Elise, "then you'd better tell me what happened at your house yesterday. It's not fair to just say shut up about it."

They had almost reached the cafeteria, where the music teacher gave the group lessons in the afternoon. Elise thought Nick was going to ignore her and march through the cafeteria door, but he paused. She asked quickly, "Did they know anything about your real parents?"

Nick hesitated before he answered, and his voice shook a little. "Yeah. Ace and Hacker—"

"Ace and Hacker?" exclaimed Elise. "Those aren't alien names."

"No." Nick sighed, as if it was too difficult to explain. "That's just what I call them to myself. Their real names are like . . . smells, with electrical signals mixed in. Ace is like old sneakers, I guess, with a jerky signal, and Hacker . . . maybe plastic. More steady. See, talking through antennae—"

"Antennae? They talk with them? *You* talked with

60

them?" Elise stood for a moment with her mouth open, trying to imagine this. "But you don't— How could you understand them?"

A man's voice, calling from inside the cafeteria, interrupted Nick and Elise's conversation. "We're waiting for you, out there. The rest of us are ready to play." It was Mr. Bell, the music teacher.

"They had a pair for me," said Nick quickly. He seemed to want to talk about it, now that he had started. "Like bionic antennae. They fit over these little bumps on my head, you know?" With his free hand, Nick brushed his hair back from one of the bumps.

"Did you used to have real antennae?" Elise shuddered a little, but she wanted to know.

"Uh-uh, they never grew." Nick's tone was as matter-of-fact as if he were talking about tadpoles' tails or something else that had nothing to do with him. "Thuban babies are born with just bumps, and then after the grown-ups have been touching them with their antennae for a year or so, the bumps grow out into baby antennae."

Elise stared at Nick's head. She didn't know whether it would be worse to have a part of you that never grew or to be the only person in the world with things like asparagus sprouting out of your hair. She thought of the wolf boy, who could never learn to talk because no human beings had talked to him when he was a baby.

"Nick and Elise, are you trying for demerits?"

Elise stepped quickly through the door, followed by

Nick. But she couldn't help asking one more question. "Those Thubans—they just happened to have an extra pair of antennae? How did they know you'd need them?"

Nick shook his head. "I don't know if they did. I think they were kind of grossed out when they saw my antenna bumps. Anyway, it's a weird kind of talking, because the words are like smells, and there's a lot I don't get."

As they reached the half circle of folding chairs, Nick shut his mouth. The other three kids with clarinets were looking on with interest, probably glad to put off the lesson for a few minutes. Mr. Bell, arms folded, was glaring at Nick and Elise. "So kind of you two to honor us with your presence."

"I'm sorry," muttered Elise as she opened her clarinet case. But she wasn't sorry at all. She was wild to know more.

The clarinet lessons were never full of beautiful music, but this one was especially bad. At the end of the half hour, Mr. Bell remarked, "Quite an achievement, kids. I don't think the five of you ever played the same note at the same time, not even once. Nor did you play any of the notes in the music in front of you."

Elise didn't care very much; clarinet lessons were one of those things, like tennis, that her mother had planned for her. She hurried down the hall after Nick. "So what about your star parents?" she asked. "Where are they?"

Nick looked down at the floor a moment before he spoke. "They're dead. There was an accident."

"Oh." Elise was shocked, and she wondered whether she should be asking Nick this private stuff. But she couldn't help going on. "How come *you* weren't killed then?"

"I already figured that out, even before I talked to Ace and Hacker." Nick looked pleased with himself, in spite of what they were talking about. "I knew I must have been left here. My mom and dad—my *Earth* mom and dad—told me a long time ago how I happened to be adopted. A guy found me at the Blue Hills ski place, in the snow. I was just a baby, not even one year old."

"Somebody left you in the snow?" asked Elise, horrified. "No, I'm sure it wasn't like that. You must have crawled out of the ship when no one was looking. You know how people always think babies won't get into trouble because they couldn't possibly push open a starship hatch or something, and then—"

"You're making all that up," said Nick angrily. "You don't know anything about it. Nobody knows anything except that this skier went down and told the ski patrol, and they came back and got me."

"But then didn't they see the ship?"

"Nope. It was dark by then. And anyway, it could have been hidden under the snow."

"But they would have found it in the spring, when the snow melted," Elise pointed out.

"It didn't stay on the Earth. The only other thing anybody knows is that the Patrol found the wreck out in space. In the asteroid belt."

A strange note had come into Nick's voice. His tone

64

made Elise imagine the abandoned baby on the ski slope, shivering and bawling inside a strange man's jacket while they slid down the trail under the darkening sky. Her eyes stung. "I bet your parents were like pioneers, and they got lost on their way to settle a new planet, and they landed here by mistake, and they had to take off again in a big hurry. And after they were up in space, they found out you were missing, and your mom and dad were really upset, and they wanted to go back to get you. But something had happened to the ship, taking off from Earth, and it was starting to fall apart, so—"

"Shut up!" exclaimed Nick. "I hate that make-believe stuff."

Elise shut up. It was hard to believe that Nick didn't want to imagine what might have happened and how. She wished she could say something to make him feel better. She had never thought that Nick's real parents might be dead. That was much worse than having them come back to take him away. Or was it?

Another question came to her mind. "Don't get mad," she told him hesitantly, "but I'm just wondering something else. What about the Thubans at your house? Are they like detectives that find missing people, or are they your relatives, or what?"

"Ace and Hacker?" They were at the classroom door now, and Nick paused with his hand on it. He frowned. "I'm not sure. They seemed really excited about finding me, but . . . maybe just because of the toothpaste. Anyway, I've got to get them to take me for a ride."

"A ride?" asked Elise uneasily. But Nick pushed open the door without saying anything else. Carrie twisted around in her seat, smiling at them meaningfully.

Nick rode Elise's bus that afternoon, and when they got off, he fell into step with her. "I had a good idea about how you could help me," he said. "You could bring over some toothpaste."

"What for?" asked Elise in amazement. "Oh—*they* want it?"

"Yeah. I don't have any money to buy more, and they asked for it about six times. They want the white kind, though, not the clear green kind."

"Okay," said Elise. "We have the white kind." She hesitated at the gate of her yard, her stomach flipping with excitement. "Can I go over there with you?"

Nick looked at her for a moment, his expression cautious, before he answered. "Maybe. We can talk about it when you bring the toothpaste."

What an adventure, thought Elise as she ran into the house. She gave her mother, talking on the kitchen telephone, a peck on the cheek. Yes, this adventure was much more exciting than any of her daydreams, because it was real. That made it scarier, too, of course. Was she really brave enough to visit the aliens with Nick?

Elise leaped up the stairs two at a time. She took the toothpaste from the bathroom she shared with Lewis, and a small tube from her father's shaving kit, and an unopened tube from her parents' medicine cabinet. That left the tube that was half full on Mom and Dad's bathroom counter. She could share with them. Lewis hardly ever brushed his teeth anyway.

Elise was about to run back down the stairs when she remembered she would have to walk past her mother carrying three tubes of toothpaste. She could put them in a plastic bag, but then her mother would wonder what was in the bag.

Then Elise had an inspiration: her clarinet case. She dashed downstairs to grab it from the kitchen table. Upstairs, she fitted in the toothpaste around the parts of the clarinet.

"Nick and I are going to practice together," Elise told her mother as she crossed the kitchen again. Her mother, still on the phone, nodded and smiled approvingly.

At Mr. Russell's front door, Nick's grandfather himself greeted her. "Hi there, sweetheart. What's this— are you and Nick starting a band?"

"Not exactly," said Elise, remembering the awful squawking of their lesson this afternoon. "We just thought we'd practice together." The only trouble with that explanation was that now she and Nick would have to play their clarinets a little, at least one piece, before they left to take the toothpaste to the aliens.

She wished Mr. Russell would let her go talk to Nick, but he stood in the doorway, putting on a serious expression. "By the way, do you know how elephants play the clarinet?"

"No, how?" asked Elise, trying to be patient.

"Not very well!" Grinning, he turned toward the back of the house. "Nick! Company for you."

7

Toothpaste
and a Space Ride

Nick met Elise in the hall and led her to the bedroom where he was staying. "Did you bring it?"

Elise opened her clarinet case and let him see her loot. Nick's eyebrows rose. "Three tubes—not bad. They should be happy with that."

"But we have to practice clarinets a little," said Elise. "I told everyone that's what we were going to do."

"That *is* bad." Nick sighed. "Well, might as well get it over with."

As they took out their instruments and stuck the pieces together, Elise gave Nick a sideways glance. Maybe *that's* why he was so terrible at playing the clarinet—because he was a star person. Elise wasn't very good, but it was because she didn't pay any attention. Nick seemed to be really trying during the lessons, but he could hardly tell the difference between one note and another. Maybe none of *them* could.

They played "Greensleeves" through twice, very fast but not exactly together. Then Elise asked, "What I don't get is, how did they know where your house was? They couldn't sense you with their antennae from the ship, could they?"

Nick laughed. "Of course not. You make them sound like aliens in a comic book. I don't know exactly how they located me, but I think Hacker found out some things that only the Patrol was supposed to know."

"Of course," said Elise eagerly. "The Patrol would watch over you, but they wouldn't let you know they were there. Like guardian angels. They were probably glad you got adopted by an Earth family, and they didn't want to interfere, but they'd keep close—"

'Jeez!" Nick gave her a disgusted glare. "Can't you stop imagining things?"

"I'm sorry," said Elise. She couldn't get it through her head that Nick really didn't like to imagine, but he didn't. She paused before she went on. "Would Ace and Hacker mind if I came with you?"

"Maybe not," said Nick slowly. "But somebody has to cover for me tonight. I thought you could do that."

"What do you mean, cover?"

"Just so nobody worries about me. See, I think Ace and Hacker will take me for a ride in the starship, but they can't take off until after dark, or somebody might see—"

"A ride?" Elise interrupted. Her stomach flipped, as though she were suddenly floating upside down, weightless. "You want to go out in space with them?"

70

"Yeah, what a chance!" Nick's eyes shone. "I never thought I'd get to travel in space until I grew up. But anyway, I can't just go out after dinner unless Grandpa thinks he knows where I am. So I thought if I said I was going to your house . . ."

"Oh, great idea," said Elise. "You have all the fun, and I tell all the lies."

"Who said you had to tell lies? That's only in case my grandfather calls up for something. You can make up an excuse." As Elise kept on staring at him, he added, "Well, you're good at making up things."

"After all the trouble I went to, getting toothpaste and everything! Forget it." Elise snapped her clarinet case shut and stood up.

"Just a minute." Nick stared at her anxiously. "You can probably come tomorrow afternoon. . . . Hey, don't you want to know where Thuban is?"

"Thuban?" Elise hesitated in the doorway. "The star that they—that you came from?"

"Yeah. Look." Nick dropped down to the carpet, where a thick encyclopedia was spread open. "It's in Draco." As Elise knelt beside him, he pointed to a small white star. "Thuban used to be the North Star in Egyptian times."

Gazing at the star map, Elise felt something shift in her mind. All this time she had been daydreaming about being a child of the stars, but she had never really thought about *where* those stars were. Now she realized with a shock that the star Thuban was a real place. A place you could go to.

When Elise and Lewis had gone to Minneapolis to visit their grandparents last year, they had driven to

71

the Boston airport and gotten on a plane and gotten off in Minneapolis. When the aliens went back to Thuban, they'd get in their starship and get out at . . . Here her imagination went blank. "What's it like on Thuban?" she asked Nick.

Nick gave her one of those looks that meant she wasn't very smart. "Nobody lives *on* Thuban. Thuban's the star—their sun. It's even hotter than our sun. They live on the second planet that orbits Thuban." He paused, and his eyes took on a faraway look. "I don't know what it's like, but I might get a chance to find out."

Elise was feeling more and more uneasy, but she didn't know what she wanted to say until she burst out with it. "Listen, I don't think you should go for that ride," she exclaimed. "Just because these aliens are from the stars, it doesn't mean they have any sense. What if you think they're taking you up in space for a little ride, but then they zoom off for Thuban?"

"Then you'd be in a lot of trouble with my grandfather," said Nick with a laugh. "Oh, come on. I've got to go! Don't you understand? A ride in a spaceship!" Nick started talking faster, and his eyes glittered as if he had a fever. "Look, it'll be easy for you to cover. Here's what I'm going to do: At exactly seven thirty, I'll leave here and walk to my house. The ride won't take that long, probably an hour. And I'll be back at Grandpa's by nine. So if he calls, all you have to do is say I'll be home in a little while, and I will."

Elise looked at him suspiciously. "Well, but—"

"Please, just cover for me this one time."

73

"All right," said Elise. "If you *promise* you'll take me with you tomorrow so I can meet them and talk to them myself."

Nick looked worried. "I don't know. Now that I think about it, they might not like it. They're too afraid of the news getting out that they're here. Anyway," he added, brightening, "you *can't* talk to them because you don't have antennae."

"Well, of course you'd have to translate for me." Elise folded her arms. "Promise, or I won't cover for you."

"Okay," said Nick with a sigh. "But *you* have to promise you won't say anything to upset them."

Elise thought this was silly, since whatever she said to the Thubans would have to be translated by Nick. But she didn't argue.

After dinner that night Elise went upstairs to do her homework. She settled herself against the pillows on her bed with a notebook and the book she was going to take notes on, *Pharaohs and UFOs.* The first picture in the book was an Egyptian painting, showing a man in a headdress facing a larger being with feelers. "An unnamed 'god' points out the North Star, Thuban, to the pharaoh," said the caption. "Note the antennas on the 'god's' head—a space helmet?"

Elise shivered. The Thubans. There they were, right here in this library book, although she was the only person in the world who knew it. Quickly she flipped the page and began to read about the Egyptian pyramids. The author seemed to think they must have been built with the help of visitors from the stars.

About eight thirty, as Elise was working on her math, the phone rang. It rang once, then twice—and then Elise remembered what she was supposed to be doing for Nick. She leaped off the bed and dashed down the hall to the phone in her parents' bedroom. "Hello?"

"I've got it, Elise," said her father's voice on the kitchen phone.

"No, *I've* got it," said Elise desperately. What a nit-wit she was. She should have been sitting in Mom and Dad's bedroom, ready to pick up the phone on the first ring. Of course, maybe this wasn't Nick's grandfather.

Then she heard Mr. Russell's laugh, with a puzzled note in it. "Actually, I can speak with Elise just as well, Fred," he told her father.

The phone downstairs clicked as Mr. Hall hung up, and Mr. Russell went on, "Just tell Nick he should be coming home pretty soon."

"All right, fine," said Elise in a rush. "Yes, he sure will." Oh, no. Nick had said he would be through with the starship ride about nine. She'd better give him a little more time. "Er, is it all right if he watches the end of this movie? It's really good."

"Movie?" Nick's grandfather sounded surprised. "I thought you two were going to work on your science projects together."

"Oh," said Elise. How was she to know what Nick had told him? "Cover for me," Nick had said, as if there was nothing to it. "Well, we did work on our projects, and now we're watching a movie. But it's almost over. Can't he please watch the end?"

"Okey-doke," said Mr. Russell, "but then he'd better scoot on home."

After she hung up, Elise went downstairs. Quietly she let herself out the back door and walked onto the lawn. It was silly to think she could see anything in the sky, not just because of the trees but because the night wasn't clear. The sky was gray with clouds, and a drop or two fell on her face.

What if she did see the starship streaking overhead again, anyway? What was she going to do—make gestures for Nick to get home? This was really silly. But Nick ought to realize he was causing a lot of trouble for her. Nick! she thought. Get on back to your grandfather's *right now.*

Indoors, her father looked around from the refrigerator as she came into the kitchen. "What were you doing outside?" He swallowed a spoonful of the stew left over from dinner.

"Oh, I just thought I might see something in the sky." Elise tried to sound dreamy and spacy. "Well, I better get back to my homework." Her father wiped his mouth, smiled, and shook his head. Before he could ask any more questions, she ran upstairs.

Elise didn't like to think that Mr. Russell might call again. But if he did, she couldn't let him talk to Mom or Dad, or even Lewis. She took her math book and paper and pencil into her parents' bedroom and sat cross-legged on their bed.

Working math problems always made Elise sleepy. Yawning, she sank back against the pillows. The nice thing about doing homework by herself was that she could drift off into a daydream now and then.

In the Hall of the Seven Galaxies, the star woman paced up and down, wringing her hands. "Even now, the boy Nick marches toward his doom. Who among us can—"

Elise jerked herself out of the daydream, alarmed. How could she let herself daydream about star people, as if nothing was wrong? What if Nick *was* marching toward his doom? She must be crazy, agreeing to cover for him while he went for a starship ride with aliens. *He* was crazy to do it.

The phone on the night table rang. Elise jumped, then grabbed it. "Hello. Hello." The time on the clock radio was 9:07.

"Isn't that movie over yet?" There was a sharp note to Mr. Russell's voice.

"No . . . not yet." Elise felt heavy with guilt. Mr. Russell had a right to know where his grandson was, especially if something had gone wrong. And Elise was the only person who could tell him.

"Come on, Elise. There's some kind of monkey business going on. Let me talk to Nick."

Elise's throat tightened with panic. Now she should tell him. But instead she blurted out, "He just left." What a stupid thing to say! If Nick didn't show up at his grandfather's within a few seconds, Mr. Russell would know that was a lie. But why hadn't Nick come back when he said he would?

"I thought you said the movie wasn't over," said Mr. Russell.

Of course he could tell something was wrong, the way she was getting mixed up. But Elise heard herself coming out with another lie. "It isn't over, but Nick thought it was getting too late anyway." She bit her lip. No. She had to tell the truth. She couldn't stand this. "Mr. Russell, there's something—"

"Whoa!" interrupted Nick's grandfather. "Here's the rascal himself, walking in the door. Just in the Nick of time, ha-ha. Take it easy, sweetheart."

As Elise listened to the click on the other end of the line, she closed her eyes and breathed out a long sigh. So Nick had not met his doom. She had been silly to worry so much. Nick didn't think the aliens were dangerous, and who would know better than he did?

"What'd you do with the toothpaste?"

Elise's eyes flew open. Lewis was standing in the door of their parents' bedroom, one hand on his hip and the other sticking his toothbrush toward her like a space ray gun.

Amazed, Elise wondered when Lewis had started brushing his teeth. But she only asked, "Isn't it in our bathroom? Anyway, you could use Mom and Dad's."

Heading for their parents' bathroom, Lewis gave her a look. "You're weird, Elise. I don't know what you're doing with that toothpaste, but you're very weird."

That night Elise dreamed that the front doorbell rang, and she answered. To her surprise, there were Nick's mother and father, with Mr. Russell standing behind them. She started to ask Nick's parents why they had come back from Bermuda so soon, but then she noticed they were all crying out loud. Not just quiet sobs—they were bawling. Screaming.

Horrified, Elise started to slam the front door shut.

But before she could move, Nick's grandfather beckoned to two policemen, who had appeared out of nowhere. "She's the one," he told the police. "It's her fault that Nick went off with the star people."

"It's not really my fault," said Elise feebly. But they handcuffed her and bundled her into the police car.

An Advanced Being

Elise woke up sweating. The morning air flowing in her window was too warm for the comforter she had needed the night before. But it was a big relief to see that she was in her bed, without handcuffs. And it was Saturday, and Nick was going to take her to see the Thubans.

Downstairs for breakfast, Elise was so glad the nightmare wasn't true that she hardly noticed the way her mother was looking at her.

"You aren't going out of the house with that rat's nest on your head, are you?" asked Mrs. Hall finally.

"I'll brush it, don't worry," said Elise carelessly. She swallowed her last bite of toast. "I'm going over to Nick's, okay?"

"Fine—*after* you brush your hair." As Elise started

for the stairs, her mother added, "By the way, Lewis says you did something with the toothpaste in your bathroom."

"Really?" Elise tried to sound completely surprised and at the same time much too busy—running upstairs to brush her hair—to discuss what might have happened to the toothpaste.

In her room, Elise's eye was caught by the book she had read last night about visitors from outer space. Nick might be interested to see the picture of that Egyptian "god," who must have really been a Thuban. Seizing the book, she pattered back downstairs.

As Elise was hurrying out the door, she noticed her mother looking at her again. Oh, no, not her hair; she couldn't stand to wait any longer. Her mother opened her mouth, but Elise slipped out and closed the door. Then she ran all the way down the road to Mr. Russell's.

Elise rang the doorbell. No answer. She thought she heard it ringing inside, but just in case, she rapped on the door several times. No answer.

Puzzled, Elise stood back from the door and looked around. Oh—Mr. Russell's car was gone from the driveway. Maybe they had gone to the store or something, and they'd be right back.

Elise sat down on the doorstep and waited for a while. It was mild enough to sit on the brick steps without a jacket, but this wasn't the peaceful kind of spring weather. Today there was a fitful, warm breeze that made Elise feel itchy and edgy.

And no blue Honda was driving back down Twin

Ponds Lane. What if Mr. Russell had dropped Nick off at Tim's for the day? Elise could sit here for hours. She'd better go home and call Tim's house.

At home Elise had to squeeze past her mother and father, who were putting the screen in the storm door. *"Elise."* Her mother's tone was quiet but dangerous-sounding. "That hair never got within three feet of a brush this morning."

"Oh, sorry," said Elise. "I'll brush it." She hurried upstairs to her parents' bedroom, looked up Tim's number in the telephone book, and called his house.

"No," said Tim's mother when Elise asked to talk to Nick, "he isn't here. Nick's grandfather took Tim and Nick to the planetarium today."

That jerk! exclaimed Elise to herself. Nick went to the planetarium, and he didn't even tell me. He wasn't even nice enough to call me this morning and tell me what was going on. After all I did for him.

"They'll be back later this afternoon," Mrs. Perillo went on. "But I don't think Nick's coming back to our house."

He'd better not, thought Elise. He said he'd take me with him to meet the Thubans, and he'd better do it.

Saturdays usually went by quickly, but not this one. Elise ended up going over to Carrie's and having lunch there and fooling around and looking at Carrie's collection of *Seventeen* magazines. But Elise kept glancing at the clock, wondering if Nick might be home yet. She called Mr. Russell's at two o'clock—no answer.

She called again at two thirty, and three—no answer.

Meanwhile, Carrie wanted to hear something juicy about Elise and Nick. "What did he say to you yesterday?"

"Nothing much," said Elise. "He showed me a star map."

"Oh-oh." Carrie rolled her eyes and started to sing an old song, "Don't Let the Stars Get in Your Eyes." She added, "By the way, Stacey told me Rosemary likes Nick, too. That's why she was being so mean."

Soon after that, Elise made some excuse about her mother wanting her home by three thirty. She didn't tell Carrie, but she was worried that maybe Mr. Russell's phone was unplugged and he didn't know it. Anyway, she had to talk to Nick the *minute* he came back.

As she turned down Twin Ponds Lane, she spotted the blue of Mr. Russell's Honda in his driveway. At last! She'd just check in with her mother, and then . . .

But at home there was an unpleasant surprise waiting for Elise. Her mother was gone, but there was a chair, with a note taped to the back of it, blocking the kitchen door. That was the way Mrs. Hall left messages for Elise when she wanted to make sure Elise got them, no matter how spacy she might be that day.

Elise—Remember our bargain? You have a 4:00 appointment at Hair, Here. I'll be home soon.

XXX Mom

P.S.: How about Chinese takeout tonight?

Oh, no. Mom had gone ahead and done it. Too late, Elise wished she had paid attention and brushed her hair. Maybe if she ran upstairs and brushed her hair good before Mom got home—

No. That wouldn't work. Elise realized now that her mother must be pretty mad at her for always promising to brush her hair and never doing it. Mom wouldn't change her mind about the haircut just because Elise finally brushed her hair at three thirty in the afternoon. Mom thought spare ribs and egg rolls would make up for having short hair.

Anyway, Elise couldn't wait any longer to talk to Nick. Taking the felt pen and note pad from the counter, Elise wrote a note to tape over the one already on the chair.

Mom—I went to Mr. Russell's. I'll be back soon.
Elise

Nobody answered Mr. Russell's doorbell, but Elise knew somebody must be home, so she opened the door. Mr. Russell waved at her from the living room, where there was a baseball game on TV. An electric organ was playing excited chords, and the crowd was yelling to the batter.

"Nick's in his room," Mr. Russell told her. "Go on in." His eyes flicked back to the TV screen. "Come on, Sox!"

The door of the bedroom Nick used was closed. Elise knocked, but she didn't wait for an answer before she opened it. "Why didn't—" she began angrily.

Then she stopped. What was Nick doing? His book bag was open on the floor. And there was a box of crackers on the bed and a tube of toothpaste beside it. Nick turned from the dresser, his mouth full of something.

"Don't eat that!" Elise gagged.

"It's pretty good," said Nick, although his mouth was pulling down as if he didn't really like it. "You should try—well, I guess you can't. You're a different life form."

Elise didn't like his tone of voice. He might as well have said, "You're a lower life form." She stood there for a moment, watching Nick stuff socks and underwear into his book bag. "Did they take you for a ride in space?"

"Yeah." Nick started laughing to himself. "Way out in space. The Earth looked like a little dot." He shook his head, still laughing. "I don't know why I didn't get it before. When I was sitting there looking out the viewer at the stars and that little dinky Earth, I finally realized—*I'm not an Earthling!*"

His words sent a cold shiver through Elise. "What do you mean?"

"I'm a Thuban. Once I get my antenna transplant, I'll be *completely* a Thuban. A star-traveler." Nick sounded very pleased with himself. "Boy, I used to be so excited about the U.S. space program—all that work and billions of dollars just to get a little shuttle in orbit around the Earth and bring it down again. Pitiful! Earthlings are so far behind, they don't have a chance of catching up to us."

85

"Us," repeated Elise. Feeling queasy, she watched Nick squeeze toothpaste on another cracker and pop it into his mouth.

"Yeah, it's pitiful." Nick tucked a few paperback books into a side pocket of his book bag. Elise glimpsed the cover of one: *1001 Riddles.* "It's like all those slaves in Egypt sweating and working for years and years to build the pyramids—just big piles of rock."

Elise felt dazed. She had come to talk to Nick, and it was as if someone else were here in his place. She found herself staring at Nick's sweatshirt, which had a picture of the Milky Way galaxy on the front. YOU ARE HERE, it said, with an arrow pointing to the rim. Finally she asked, "Why didn't you tell me you were going to the planetarium? I came over this morning, and no one was home."

"Oh, the planetarium," said Nick scornfully. He didn't seem to notice that Elise was annoyed at him. "What a laugh. The program was about exploring the solar system, and they made a big deal about their special effects and how you'd feel just like you were in a spaceship." He laughed again. "Oh, well. At least I talked the old man into buying me a good sweat shirt there. I got T-shirts like this for Ace and Hacker, too."

"You told your grandfather the T-shirts were for Ace and Hacker?" asked Elise hopefully. If his grandfather already knew, she would feel better.

"No," said Nick, stuffing the T-shirts into his bag. "I told him they were for my Earth parents."

The way Nick was talking about "the old man" and his "Earth parents" made Elise uncomfortable, but she didn't think it was any of her business. She asked casually, "So the books and socks and stuff are for the Thubans, too?"

Nick looked at her in surprise. "Why would they want my underwear?"

"But—" Elise swallowed. "You mean you're going with them." Her voice rose. "You can't go that far away by yourself!" That sounded stupid, so she went on quickly. "You've got to tell somebody, like your grandfather. Or your parents."

"Don't be dumb." Nick smiled his superior smile. "They wouldn't believe me, and they wouldn't let me go if they did. But anyway, I'll probably only be gone a couple of weeks."

Elise felt caught in a nightmare that was coming true. "What makes you think the Thubans will bring you back? It's dangerous for them."

"Dangerous?" Nick smiled his advanced-being smile again. "Space travel isn't dangerous for Thubans. You see, we developed interstellar flight long ago, and now a trip from their planet to Earth is as easy as—"

"That's not what I mean," Elise interrupted. "I mean the Patrol might get them. I bet they wouldn't want to take a chance on that."

Nick didn't seem to be paying attention to what she was saying. Zipping his book bag shut, he stood up. "Guess that's all I need." He heaved the bag onto one shoulder and turned toward the door. "See you."

"Just a minute!" Elise was getting angry. "Just because you're an advanced being, it doesn't mean you have to act like a jerk. You promised me I could come along today and talk to Ace and Hacker."

"Oh, yeah." Turning back to Elise, Nick looked worried. "Do you have to? It might ruin everything for me. And it wouldn't be that great for you because you couldn't talk to them yourself." He backed toward the door.

"Maybe they could give me bionic feelers, like they did you."

"Nope," answered Nick without hesitating. "It's not just the antennae; it's the part of the brain that you understand them with. Only advanced beings have that."

"Oh, right," said Elise sarcastically. "Excuse *me*. Anyway, I have to get my hair cut now. But I'll come over to your house afterward, okay?"

"I guess so." Nick stepped through the doorway, glancing toward the living room, where the baseball game was still on TV. "Better come before dark, though. That's when we have to leave."

"Evans," they heard Mr. Russell shout at the TV, "you're still the best!"

The front door clicked quietly as Nick opened it and clicked quietly shut behind him. Elise started to follow him, then stopped. She wished Nick had offered to wait until she got her hair cut, but obviously he hadn't wanted to wait. She would have felt better about going to see the aliens *with* Nick, instead of meeting him there.

Elise stepped back into the bedroom Nick had left. The encyclopedia was open on the floor. There was Thuban. Looking at the star map made her feel confused and scared, but also excited. Maybe *I* could travel to the stars, she found herself thinking. Not just daydream, but really do it.

Then she caught sight of Nick's blue NASA shirt hanging over the back of a chair. Somehow that shirt worried her. She wished he had taken it with him.

Nick was wrong to go off with the aliens without telling anyone. And his talk about an antenna transplant was sickening. And if Elise didn't want it to be her fault, she ought to tell. Tell Mr. Russell?

Through the bedroom window Elise noticed a Jeep pulling up in front of the house, and a horn tooted twice. Mom, ready to take Elise to the hairdresser. "Rats!" said Elise out loud. But she was glad she didn't have to try to tell Nick's grandfather now. Maybe later.

Elise ran out the door, calling to Mr. Russell. "That's my mom. Bye!" He gave her a wave without taking his eyes off the game.

A short while later, Elise sat under a large fern in the waiting room of Hair, Here. She watched the minute hand of the wall clock edging forward, and she worried about whether she was going to have time to go to Nick's house. Elise was supposed to walk home after her haircut, and then her mother was going to take her to the video store to rent a movie for tonight and to the Chinese takeout place to get food for supper.

The time for Elise to go meet the aliens, of course, was after her haircut, before she went home. She could tell Mom afterward that the hairdresser had run late.

The trouble was, the hairdresser *was* running late. Mom might even come to Hair, Here before Elise's haircut was over, to see what was taking so long and to pick her up before she could leave by herself. If Mom did, that would be the end of Elise's chance to meet the Thubans.

Elise sighed and squirmed and tried to keep her mind off the minutes sliding by. The jungly plants and steamy air in the hairdresser's made her think of India, and of the TV program she had seen a few days ago about the wolf boy.

There was one scene, especially, that came to Elise's mind as clearly as if she were watching it on TV again. It showed the wolf family at their den and the father wolf coming back from hunting. Each pup, in its turn, crouched low in front of the father, and the father pretended to bite its muzzle. Even though the wolf boy didn't look anything like a wolf pup, he crouched down, too, and the wolf father pretended to bite his nose. Then the father and mother rested while the pups and the boy played, rolling around on the grass in front of the den.

In a way, that boy looked terrible—all crusted with dirt, his hair long and matted. But he was grinning as he tumbled around with the wolf pups, and his eyes shone.

Now the bad feeling from that program came back to Elise, worse than ever. For some reason, it seemed very important for her to go to Nick's and actually *see* him with the aliens. Then she would know. . . . She couldn't sit here any longer.

The bad feeling pushed Elise to her feet. In the big mirror in the next room, the hairdresser caught her eye and called, "Be with you in a minute here, Elise."

Elise nodded and smiled and sat down again. But as soon as the hairdresser bent over to pick up a roller, she slipped out the door.

Alien or Human?

It was only a couple of blocks from Hair, Here to the school. From there, Elise trotted up Mallard Street and along the edge of the golf course. This was the way Nick normally walked home after school, instead of riding Elise's bus to his grandfather's.

It couldn't be too late, she told herself as she hurried along the path, keeping an eye out for golf balls flying from the other side of the fairway. Nick said they wouldn't leave until dark, and it was only about four thirty. No—actually, he'd said they might leave *before* sunset if the Thubans got worried. And what if they'd already gone into the ship and wouldn't come out?

Under the shade of the pine trees, Elise listened to the warm breeze sighing through the branches like restless breathing. She thought of the aliens, or rather tried *not* to think of how scared she'd been the first time she saw them. Those blank faces, and the twitching antennae above them. If Nick went to Thuban, he would be around them all the time.

A vision came to Elise of Nick standing in a crowd of Thubans, their antennae like a field of waving asparagus. A tape clicked on in her head.

Halfway across the galaxy, the boy Nick stood at last on the surface of the planet Thuban. He searched the crowd around him for a friendly face, but all the faces were blank. Above each blank face sprouted a pair of antennae.

Too late he realized his mistake. Now there was only one—the brave girl from Earth—who could rescue him from a life of dreary exile.

The trouble was, once Nick got to Thuban, it really would be too late. If Elise was going to rescue him, she would have to do it here and now.

Elise had reached the shrubs at the edge of Nick's lawn. She paused to catch her breath, looking across the lawn to the house.

She froze. The sliding door was opening.

One of the Thubans, wearing a T-shirt, peered carefully around the yard before he stepped out. His antennae, like two brown asparagus stalks, waved back and forth as if they were helping him inspect the yard.

Next came the second alien, much shorter, wearing jeans and a sweatshirt and carrying a book bag. Then another Thuban in a T-shirt, not quite as tall as the first. The third Thuban was wearing something around his neck—a pendant, like a crystal, as big as an egg.

Wait a minute. *Three* Thubans? There were only supposed to be two.

94

The short alien was Nick.

Elise shrank back, as if she had rushed up to the edge of a cliff and almost stepped over it. *Nick is an alien.* All her worry about him melted away, and she wanted to run.

"Elise!" Nick shaded his eyes against the afternoon sun, squinting toward the woods. "Get out of here! It's too late."

The sound of his voice made Elise's vision of Nick shift sharply, like one of those trick pictures of a box. If you look at it one way, you see the outside of the box. Move your eyes just a little, and you're looking at the inside. That alien was only Nick, the boy she knew, with bionic feelers fastened on his head.

"You said I could meet them!" she shouted back. "You promised." Part of her mind was still urging, Run! But she marched forward across the lawn until she was only a few yards from the deck. She could see now that the antennae on top of Nick's head moved jerkily, and they were gray rather than brown like the others'.

Nick was leaning over the railing, glaring at her. The two Thubans stood by the door, as empty-faced as store-window mannikins. But their antennae were touching, and Elise heard a faint crackling noise, like someone else's tape player turned down low. She shivered. They're talking like ants, she thought.

"You can't stay," said Nick. "The Patrol is coming around sooner than they thought, so we have to finish filming and leave."

"Filming?" Elise thought he must be joking. "You mean they're making a *movie* here?"

"Not exactly a movie, of course," said Nick impatiently. "I said 'filming,' but it's much more advanced and realistic than that. A movie is just the closest thing to what they're making."

"And it's all about wonderful you, I suppose," said Elise. "But I don't care. I covered for you last night, and you promised—"

She broke off as the taller Thuban tapped Nick on the shoulder, and Nick turned to touch antennae with him. There was that crackling noise again. Nick's mouth dropped open and his eyes glazed over, as if he were trying to listen to very faint music.

Then Nick turned back to her, his eyes still a little unfocused. "Okay," he said.

"Okay what?"

"Okay, Ace says you can ask a couple of questions if you help out with the filming first." He walked down the steps of the deck, followed by the two Thubans. The shorter alien—it must be Hacker—held up his crystal pendant toward Elise.

"Hi," said Elise to the Thubans, feeling a little foolish as they watched her with smooth faces. Only their antennae twitched and turned like dogs' ears. "What do they mean, help with the filming?" she went on to Nick.

"Bite my arm," he said, holding his forearm out toward her.

"What?" Elise wondered if his brain was scrambled from all that talking with antennae.

"Not really, stupid. Just pretend. Ace wants a scene of savage Earth life. Go ahead and do it, and then they'll talk to you."

"I thought you *hated* pretending," said Elise. She glanced at the aliens, standing at the bottom of the steps. Hacker was still holding up the crystal in their direction. Savage Earth life, huh?

Well, if that's what they wanted— She grabbed Nick's arm and bared her teeth, pretending to sink them into his flesh. Nick let out a horrible noise, something between a scream and a groan.

Startled, Elise jumped back. Then she saw that Hacker was right behind her with his crystal, and she edged off to one side. He smelled like a plastic air mattress.

"All right?" Elise asked Nick. "Now you have to help me talk to them."

Nick sighed before he answered. "Look, you got to meet them, didn't you? We have to leave now. Besides, I can tell you a lot more about Thuban in a couple of weeks, when I come back."

His last words made Elise shudder, thinking of the antenna transplant. "No. *Now.*"

With a shrug, Nick stepped up to Hacker and touched the ends of his antennae to the Thuban's. The trancelike look came over Nick's face again.

"Ask them why they want to take you back to Thuban," commanded Elise.

"I know *that* without asking them," said Nick. "They want to rescue me from a life of savagery among backward life forms."

"Go ahead and ask them," insisted Elise.

Nick stood still for a moment with his antennae grazing Hacker's and the question crackling between them. Hacker's eyes looked in Elise's direction, but without any expression. Then Nick spoke slowly, in a tone like someone hypnotized. "Youngling goes to other existence in Thuban system."

"See?" asked Nick in his regular voice. "Hacker told you just what I told you."

Elise stared at Nick. "No, he didn't. It wasn't the same at all. You said—" She stopped. It was no use arguing with Nick. But maybe she could talk the Thubans out of taking him. "Never mind. Ask them— aren't they afraid the Patrol will get them if they try to take you from the Earth?"

Without moving, Nick let his eyes glaze over again, and something sizzled between his antennae and Hacker's. Hacker's answer came out of Nick's mouth in a flat voice: "Once Earth boy in Thuban system, Patrol has no power."

Elise felt a chill. "Why are they calling you Earth boy?"

A puzzled look crept over Nick's face, but he answered, "Why not? I'm the only Thuban who's lived on the Earth, aren't I?"

Elise sighed and squeezed her hands together. She felt she was close to getting the truth, but she had to get it out of the Thubans. "Okay. Ask them—ask them, after you get your antenna transplant, will you be just like a regular Thuban?"

"I thought I already told you I would." Nick looked annoyed, but he stretched his antennae toward Hacker's again. As Nick's question and Hacker's answer crackled back and forth, Nick looked mystified and uneasy. "Maybe no transplant," he reported Hacker's answer. "If Earth boy turns Thuban, not interesting."

"Nick!" Elise burst out. "Don't you see? You'll be like the wolf boy. You'll never fit in."

Pulling his antennae away from Hacker's, Nick glared at Elise. "What are you talking about, won't fit in? I'm a Thuban. Just more interesting because I grew up here, that's all."

"Yeah, you'll be interesting, all right," said Elise. "You'll be a freak." The vision of Nick among the Thubans reappeared in her mind, and she felt she would be sick right there on the lawn if she didn't tell him. "Listen! *Halfway across the galaxy, the boy Nick stood at last on the surface of the planet Thuban.*"

"I told you, Thuban isn't the planet, it's the star," said Nick. "Can't you even get that right?"

"*—of the planet circling the star Thuban,*" Elise went on. She didn't care how stupid Nick thought she was if she could only get this out. "*He searched the crowd around him for a friendly face, but all the faces were blank. Above each blank face waved a pair of asparagus-like antennae. Nick's own antennae bumps ached, and he longed to take off his bionic pair. But the only way to talk to anyone here was through these insect parts. Clutching his book bag, the little bit of Earth he had brought with him, Nick was seized with a desire to tell someone a riddle. And his heart ached, because he knew that a chasm of many light years cut him off from anyone who would understand a riddle.*"

100

Elise paused. She squeezed her eyes shut and opened them again. She didn't feel sick anymore, just empty and foolish.

"Oh, boy," said Nick with disgust. "You and your imagination. Where do you get all that longing and heart-aching stuff? Don't worry, I'm going to fit in fine once I get to Thuban. I *am* Thuban, remember?"

"What about riddles?" demanded Elise. "Why'd you bring your riddle book?"

For a moment Nick looked stumped. But then he said scornfully, "You don't know what you're talking about. Where'd you get the idea they can't understand riddles?"

Elise didn't know. It had just felt right. "Okay, then, *ask* them a riddle. See if they get it."

As soon as she said this, Elise was so anxious that she had to bite the insides of her cheeks. It seemed logical that people with blank faces wouldn't think riddles were funny—but she didn't know.

Nick snorted. "All right, just to show you. What riddle?"

"Well . . ." Naturally, now Elise couldn't think of any. "Your grandfather told me one. 'How do elephants play the clarinet?' And the answer is 'Not very well.' "

Nick rolled his eyes as if he had heard that riddle more than once, but he touched antennae with Hacker again. Elise squeezed her hands together hard. For all she knew, the Thubans told riddles morning, noon, and night. If she was wrong about this, Nick wouldn't listen to her anymore.

"Uh—" Nick had an uneasy look in his eyes. "That riddle wasn't very good. What's another one?"

Elise felt a rush of hope, but her mind went blank. She had heard dozens of riddles at school during the last few weeks. It was a fad that Tim had started, and he had told the most. But everyone, even Mrs. Curley, had told riddles. She looked around the yard, hoping to see something that would remind her of one of them.

The taller Thuban stepped close to Nick and Hacker and joined his antennae with theirs. Nick muttered, "No more time for questions. Patrol approaching."

"Wait!" Elise had been staring at the house, and something had come to her. "Ask them—tell them you can jump higher than your house."

A faint smile twitched Nick's mouth. "Because the house can't jump, you mean."

"Yes."

Elise bit her cheeks again as the riddle crackled from Nick's antennae to the Thubans'. This was her last chance to rescue Nick.

"They didn't get it." Nick sounded dazed. His antennae pulled away from Ace and Hacker's, drooping like floppy rabbit ears. "They just didn't get it."

"But *you* did," exclaimed Elise. "Because you're a human being." I won! she thought. She wanted to jump higher than the house herself. "Ask them one more question." She was almost shouting. "If you go with them to Thuban, can you come back?"

Nick's gray antennae twitched toward Hacker, then flopped over again. Fear flashed across his face. "I don't think I'd better . . ." He took a step toward Elise.

Suddenly Elise felt she couldn't stand there one more minute, so close to Ace and Hacker's creepy blank faces. "Run!"

Nick leaned forward, his arms doubled up as if to break into a sprint. Elise was about to turn and dash for the woods when she saw that he had stopped. "Come on!" she urged. "Before they grab you."

Ace and Hacker stood quietly in back of Nick, their arms at their sides. Then why wasn't Nick moving? Why was he leaning backward now?

It was their antennae. The aliens' antennae were aimed toward Nick's, crackling like Fourth of July sparklers. Nick was trapped by the two Thubans, as helpless as if his finger were stuck in a light socket. With Ace on one side of Nick and Hacker on the other, the three of them turned slowly and began walking toward the swimming pool.

"No, don't go!" Even as she was screaming, Elise could see that Nick couldn't help it. She started after them, thinking wildly that she would do *something*, like tripping one of the Thubans. Then she caught a whiff of Ace's smell, like Lewis's old sneakers, but worse. She shrank back, her knees turning to jelly.

As Elise watched with her fists pressed to her mouth, not daring to get any closer, Hacker peeled one corner of the swimming pool cover back from the glossy ship. A hatch opened. Ace lowered himself in and pulled Nick down. Hacker climbed into the open-

103

ing. For an instant his antennae waved above the hatch, and then he disappeared after the others. The hatch closed.

Nick the Earth boy was gone.

The Return
of the Earth Boy

"No!" Elise lunged toward the pool, dropped to her knees on the slick surface of the ship, and scrabbled with her fingernails at the place where the hatch had opened. She couldn't even see a line.

Elise pushed herself backward onto the lawn again, gasping for breath through her tight throat. Run for help.

What help? No neighbors close by. Home, or Mr. Russell's house, or even the golfers on the golf course, too far away. Ship might take off any minute. Right now!

Stop them.

How? Elise felt cold and hollow. If she were a heroic child of the stars, it would be easy. In her daydreams, Elise saved entire worlds.

But right now, right here, she couldn't save even

one friend. She couldn't hold the ship down with her bare hands, could she?

Hold it down. What if she got a lot of heavy things and piled them on top of the swimming pool cover? Maybe that would keep the ship from taking off.

Something heavy. A big pile of dirt? Get a shovel from the garage, dig—

No. Elise stopped herself halfway to the garage. Shoveling dirt would take too long. What else was heavy, something she could carry quickly? Furniture, from inside the house?

Elise had bounded up the deck steps and was almost at the sliding door when she saw the deck furniture. A redwood picnic table and benches, armchairs . . .

Panting in loud gasps, Elise dragged an armchair across the deck, bumped it down the steps, dragged it across the lawn. She knew the legs were gouging furrows in the grass, but she could explain later to Nick's parents.

She hauled the chair up onto the swimming pool cover. She felt the ship humming under her feet, through the plastic, and her stomach twisted. They're getting ready to leave, she thought. Hurry. Hurry!

Trying to ignore the awful gasping noise she was making, Elise jumped onto the grass and ran back to the deck. The table was the heaviest thing. Too heavy for her to move. But she *was* moving it, pulling it by the legs. Tipping it sideways and shoving it down the steps. Hauling it, a few inches at a time, across the lawn.

As Elise yanked the picnic table up onto the bulge

of the swimming pool cover, she thought the humming under her feet had gone up a notch. More weight! *Hurry.*

But her legs and arms were trembling so hard that Elise paused, leaning on the back of the redwood armchair. Rest a moment, then make another run to the deck.

As she stood with her head hanging, gazing blankly at the exposed curve of the ship, she realized that the dark surface was changing.

The hatch was opening again.

There was a thin new-moon slice of a circle, then a quarter circle, as if a manhole cover were sliding sideways. Elise's heart thumped, and a new burst of energy surged through her. With her mouth open, grunting like a pig, she began to drag the armchair over the widening hole. Quick! Quick, before antennae snaked through the hatch and alien hands reached out to grab her!

But it was a furry head *without* antennae that popped out of the ship. A boy's hands grasped the edge of the hole to boost himself out.

"Nick!"

He crouched on the slippery outside of the ship, staring from Elise to the armchair she was still gripping. "What're you doing? Are you crazy?"

Elise shook her head, not because she wasn't crazy but because it was just too much to explain. Then she screamed and pointed—antennae were poking out of the hatch.

"Go!" shouted Nick. He reached over and pinched

both antennae hard. Elise leaped onto the lawn, Nick scrambled to the edge of the pool, and they both dashed for the woods.

Elise just ran, not daring to look back. But as they reached the shrubs at the edge of the lawn, Nick threw a glance over his shoulder. "Hey, look," he panted. "They aren't chasing us. Watch this."

Elise stopped and turned just in time to see the furniture on top of the pool cover jiggling like buildings in an earthquake. Then there was a loud ripping noise. A shape like a gigantic black double Frisbee burst through the cover, straight up into the air. The picnic table and armchair flew off onto the lawn. *Crash. Crash.*

"Uh-oh," said Nick.

Elise felt foolish. So much for trying to be a hero. "I'm sorry," she said.

Nick shrugged, looking worried. "We might not be safe yet, you know." He glanced up into the trees. "Maybe they're going to hang up there and pick us off when we come out of the woods."

Elise wished he hadn't said that. As she followed Nick along the path through the pines, she tried not to think of what might be gliding above the treetops. She breathed in the smells of pine needles and damp earth, and she wondered if Nick was glad to be smelling this fresh air instead of the Thuban scents of old sneakers and air mattress inside the starship.

Ahead of her, Nick put a hand on the top of his head. "Ow, ow, *ow,*" he muttered.

"What?" asked Elise. "Your antennae?"

"Yeah. It kills to just pull them off like I did. But I had to, to get away."

"Yes. They were holding you prisoner with the powerful beams of energy from their antennae." Elise spoke breathlessly to Nick's back. "Imagine their rage and disbelief when you ripped—"

"It wasn't like that," said Nick without turning around. "They let me go so they could work the ship's controls, and I just pulled off the antennae. By the time they noticed, I was almost out the hatch."

At the edge of the woods Nick paused, putting out a hand behind him to warn Elise to stop. They both tipped their heads back, peering through the branches for a dark, round shape.

We should have Nick's binoculars now, thought Elise. Then she drew in her breath sharply. She didn't need binoculars to recognize that round shape far up in the sky. To anyone who didn't know, it would be only a darker spot in the dark cloud. But Elise knew it was the Thuban ship, waiting like a hawk to pounce on two mice as they scurried across the golf course.

"We're in deep marshmallow now," Nick muttered. "Well, they can't get us as long as we stay in the woods." But he didn't sound too certain.

Fear choked Elise's throat. She imagined a giant vacuum tube reaching down from the ship, sucking up the two of them along with a few trees. Was the Thuban ship sinking lower, closer?

Then a disk of cool white light, like a tiny moon, slid between the cloud and the dark spaceship. *Snap*—the white circle ate up the dark one. *Flash*—both circles

110

were gone. A noise like thunder rumbled overhead.

Elise and Nick lowered their faces from the empty sky and stared at each other. "That was the Patrol!" Elise was sure she was right. "They'll haul those outlaw aliens off to an Interstellar Court and have a big trial, and Ace and Hacker will have to pay dearly for transgressing the Law of the Galaxy. They'll be sentenced to long exiles on a desert planet, so that they'll never have a chance to return to Earth and bother—"

Elise stopped, feeling silly. Nick was grinning at her. "Well, you're safe now, anyway," she ended lamely.

"Maybe," said Nick. He rubbed the top of his head again, wincing. "I don't really know anything about the Patrol, like what their ship would look like, or what they would do to Ace and Hacker. But I guess that could have been them."

Snorting in disbelief, Elise shook her head. "Okay, maybe there won't be a big trial. But how can you say that wasn't the Patrol catching Ace and Hacker? What do you think it was, a funny-shaped bolt of lightning?"

"I just don't think we should jump to conclusions," said Nick in his reasonable tone. "I *said* you might be right. Anyway, I guess we don't have to hide in the woods anymore."

Elise and Nick were silent as they trudged along the golf cart path. The late afternoon sun slanted across the marsh, casting their shadows taller than the shadows of the reeds. Elise wished they had a golf cart to ride in; her legs and arms and back ached from moving that heavy furniture. But she didn't complain, because she was embarrassed. What a nitwit, trying to

111

keep a starship down by piling things on top of it. Worse, she had almost shut Nick inside the ship.

Elise walked on, her legs trembling with every step, up the rise to the last tee before Mallard Street. They were still a long way from home. After they crossed the street, they would still have to walk all the way past the tennis courts and across the rest of the golf course and down to the ponds and Twin Ponds Lane.

Elise groaned and sank onto a bench. "I'm not going any farther." She noticed a robin bouncing across the fairway as if it had springs in its skinny legs, and she felt even more tired. "When you get to your grandfather's, call my mom and tell her where I am, okay?"

Without answering, Nick pointed toward the road. Elise looked around to see a car pulling onto the grass.

The car was a Jeep. Its driver was rolling down the window.

"Elise! Where have you been? Get in the car!"

Mom's voice, angrier than Elise had ever heard it. At that sound, Elise got to her feet and staggered down the hill to the road.

"You too, Nick," Mrs. Hall went on in a grim tone. "Do you know how *frantic* we've been? Especially after your grandfather checked at your house just now and discovered the vandalism. How could you—"

"We saw it, too," said Elise in a small voice as she climbed into the car. "We were scared that the—the vandals might come after us."

"That's why we were hiding in the woods," said Nick in his most sensible tone from the backseat.

But Mrs. Hall laughed shortly. "I'm sure Nick's parents wouldn't want either of you at his house in the first place while they're away." Her voice trailed off, making Elise glance sideways at her mother. Mom's lips trembled as she went on in a much lower tone. "I was on my way to the police station."

Elise was shocked by the expression on her face. Mom, who always had things under control, looked so helpless. She was really scared that something had happened to me, thought Elise. In a burst of remorse, she exclaimed, "I'll get my hair cut tomorrow, Mom!"

"You certainly will," snapped her mother.

That was a sobering thought, and for a moment Elise rode along in silence. But then happiness welled up in her throat. Here she was in the Jeep, instead of in the Thuban starship. And so was Nick. She *had* rescued him. She had done it!

Elise managed to choke down a chortle, but she couldn't resist turning to whisper to Nick. "I guess we're in deep marshmallow."

Late the next afternoon, Sunday, Elise was looking in the bathroom mirror. Tilting her head back, she tried to pretend that her hair was longer than it really was. The hairdresser certainly had shaped it up, all right. Mom might call this medium length, but Elise called it short. And she hated it.

Downstairs the doorbell rang. "Elise!" Lewis yelled up at her.

Elise came down, still pulling the ends of her hair to try to make them longer, and found Nick standing on the porch steps. He was looking off down the road, as if he wasn't sure why he was here.

"Hi," said Elise.

"Hi," said Nick. Then, in surprise, "Wow. You really got your hair cut."

"Believe me, it wasn't my idea." Elise glanced at his own furry hair, then away.

Nick winced, as if he knew what she was thinking. "At least no one's ever going to make me get my hair cut because it's too long."

"How come you're still at your grandfather's?" asked Elise. "I thought your mom and dad were coming back from Bermuda today."

"They are," said Nick gloomily. "I'm waiting for them."

"Are you going to tell them what happened?" As Nick just looked at her, she added quickly, "I guess you can't."

"I wish I could, though." Nick sighed deeply. "Then I'd know."

Know what? Elise opened her mouth to ask, but shut it again. What Nick wanted to know was, would his parents still want him if they knew he was an alien?

"I wanted to go back to the house and clean up some before they came home," Nick went on. "Ace and Hacker left blobs of toothpaste and cracker crumbs all over."

"Want me to go with you?" offered Elise. "Maybe we could put the deck furniture back, too, and patch it together a little."

Nick smiled for the first time. "Put all the splinters in a neat pile, you mean? Anyway, I can't go anywhere." He gestured down the road, to where Mr. Russell sat on his front steps, smoking his pipe.

114

"Grandpa won't let me out of his sight until Mom and Dad pick me up."

"I'm sure they won't blame you for the mess," said Elise, but she knew that wasn't what Nick was worried about. As she tried to think of something cheerful to say, a station wagon turned onto the gravel road. In the front seat were a man and a woman, looking very tanned. "There they are."

Nick turned and walked slowly toward the gate. The station wagon passed Elise's house, but then stopped in the middle of the road, and Nick ran out to it. The doors popped open, and his mother and father climbed out, their faces beaming.

Elise couldn't hear what they said, but she saw Nick's father pretend to punch his nose, then put an arm around his shoulders. His mother kissed him and rumpled his furlike hair.

Elise thought of the scene in the wolf boy program when the wolf boy was still living with the pack, and the wolf father greeted him in front of the den. Her throat hurt. Feeling that she was watching something too private, she went back in the house.

- 11 -

Quite a Project

At school, a few days later, Mrs. Curley handed back the science reports. "Some of you did very nice work on your enrichment projects," said Mrs. Curley, walking around the classroom. "For instance"—she beamed at Rosemary and held up a paper with a red A on it before she set it down on Rosemary's desk—"this one, 'Solid Waste Disposal.' Rosemary really dug into the subject. Good going!"

Carrie leaned over from her desk to whisper loudly to Elise. "So *that's* why she smells—she dug into it."

Elise giggled. She happened to remember that Rosemary's big sister had done a science fair project on waste disposal a couple of years ago, and she was pretty sure that Rosemary hadn't done all that work over again herself.

The teacher went on around the room with the reports. Elise heard Tim say, "Hey, Russell. You got your NASA shirt on."

Elise turned in surprise. Why hadn't she noticed that? Sure enough, Nick was wearing the blue short-sleeved shirt with NASA on the front. He looked good in it.

Tim went on, "Hey, did you know that NASA was going to put a restaurant on the moon?"

"Don't be dumb," said Nick, but he smiled.

"I'm serious!" said Tim. "The food might be good, but the restaurant won't have any *atmosphere.*"

Nick groaned and laughed. Then he said, "That reminds me, I'm so mad—someone took my riddle book."

I know who, thought Elise. She had seen Nick walk to the spaceship with his book bag on his back and climb out of the hatch without it. So Nick's book bag was in the Thuban ship, which had been swallowed by the Patrol ship.

She imagined the Patrol starship streaking through the galaxy, past star clusters and planets with rings and double moons and black holes. Inside the ship, Ace and Hacker slouched against a wall in handcuffs and leg irons. The Patrol officers, their antennae crackling with puzzlement, pored over the riddle book and tried on Nick's socks.

Then she forgot about Thuban as the teacher set a paper on her desk. Mrs. Curley made a reproachful clucking noise with her tongue. "Elise. I asked you to stick to the facts. You had many interesting ideas, but you needed facts from your reading and your observa-

tions. We talked about that in class, remember?" The red letter at the top of Elise's paper was a B—.

"Now, Nick." The teacher stepped past Elise's desk and shook a paper in front of him. "*You* gave plenty of facts about meteors, and it was good to include your research at the planetarium. But you simply didn't tie your facts together with ideas."

Elise twisted around in her seat to see what grade Nick had gotten. The red letter on his paper was a B—, too. His gaze caught hers, and he grinned a big human grin.

Looking from Nick to Elise and back again, the teacher shook her head sadly. "I still think if the two of you had teamed up, it would have been quite a project."